Never Make a Bet with a Betty

"Without the protection of your gilded Beverly Hills existence, you'd be completely lost, Cher," Josh said.

"As if! I would not be lost. Daddy says I am way directionally enhanced. I am totally equipped to deal with any world. Gilded or matte. Whatever."

"Really." Josh had this new tone in his voice. Know-it-all mixed with bemused. "Prove it. I bet you can't make it thirty days without your credit cards, without your cell phone. Let's see if you can get and keep a paying job—for one month."

I stuck out my chin. "You know what? You are so on, Josh. I hereby accept your challenge—with a few caveats." I used to think caveats went best with crackers, but now I know it means conditions.

"Name them." Josh faced me full on.

"Okay, if I win—which, hello! I will—this is what I want: college Baldwins. Three, because I want a selection."

Clueless™ Books

CLUELESS™
A novel by H. B. Gilmour
Based on the film written and directed by Amy Heckerling

CLUELESS™: CHER'S GUIDE TO . . . WHATEVER
By H. B. Gilmour

CLUELESS™: ACHIEVING PERSONAL PERFECTION
By H. B. Gilmour

CLUELESS™: AN AMERICAN BETTY IN PARIS
By Randi Reisfeld

CLUELESS™: CHER NEGOTIATES NEW YORK
By Jennifer Baker

CLUELESS™: CHER'S FURIOUSLY FIT WORKOUT
By Randi Reisfeld

CLUELESS™: FRIEND OR FAUX
By H. B. Gilmour

CLUELESS™: CHER GOES ENVIRO-MENTAL
By Randi Reisfeld

CLUELESS™: BALDWIN FROM ANOTHER PLANET
By H. B. Gilmour

CLUELESS™: TOO HOTTIE TO HANDLE
By Randi Reisfeld

Available from ARCHWAY Paperbacks

Too Hottie to Handle

Randi Reisfeld

AN ARCHWAY PAPERBACK
Published by POCKET BOOKS
New York   London   Toronto   Sydney   Tokyo   Singapore

AN ARCHWAY PAPERBACK *Original*

An Archway Paperback published by
POCKET BOOKS, a division of Simon & Schuster Inc.
1230 Avenue of the Americas, New York, NY 10020

™ and Copyright © 1997 by Paramount Pictures

ISBN: 0-671-01160-X

First Archway Paperback printing June 1997

10 9 8 7 6 5 4 3 2 1

AN ARCHWAY PAPERBACK and colophon are
registered trademarks of Simon & Schuster Inc.

Printed in the U.S.A.

IL: 7+

Acknowledgments

In today's *Final Jeopardy!* the category is:

*"The people who helped make this book
so doable."*

WHO ARE . . .
The **A**-Team: **A**rchway's **A**nne Greenberg and
Amira Rubin, and always, **A**gent Fran Lebowitz of
Writers House, and . . .

The **T**-Team: the **t**otally **t**ubular **t.b.** contingent
who are *so* top drawer, top shelf, and over the top,
too . . .

And The **H**ome Team: Marvin, Scott, and Stefanie,
for the input, output, and putting up with me!
(Okay, you too, Peabo.)

Too Hottie to Handle

Chapter 1

*N*ights like this are totally golden. It's like that famous poem about form following function. My form was fully swathed in the sartorial equivalent of comfort food: DKNY drawstring sweats, fuzzy panda slippers, an '80s cut-off sweatshirt, like the *Flashdance* Betty wore. My happy face was a beguiling pastiche of exfoliant topped with intense hydrating herbal mask. It was the exact shade of olivey sage green as the voluptuous soft leather couch I was sunk deeply into.

My function was elegantly simple. Thursday is total put-it-on-pause day, the one that comes between the random bustle of my weekday activities and the full and furious swirl of my weekend agenda. The aura of our house followed the form and the function. That is, the entire staff, including our housekeeper, Lucy, had the night off.

My best friend, De, and I were massively engaged in our new and instantly classic weekly tradition, watching vintage reruns of *90210: The Lost Episodes*. It's all Luke Perry as Dylan before the receding hairline, Shannen Doherty as Brenda before she got fired, and Tori Spelling with shoulder-length hair in that garish platinum hue.

"This is such a way cleansing ritual, a reminder of simpler times," De was saying as she chomped loudly on a Dorito. At least I think it was a Dorito. I couldn't actually eyeball it, as De and I were ensconced in our separate abodes, communing via cell phone.

De was so right. Life *was* simpler back then. All we had to think about was clothes. Now it's clothes, cars, cellulars, credit cards, and Baldwins.

"Remember, Cher, when Shannen wore that dress in the first season?" De was reminiscing about the scene being played out on the TV.

"And how Amber, a fashion victim in training, at the tender age of ten, went out and copied it, viciously underestimating the size differential between Tween Dresses and Teen Formals," I finished De's thought. Together we both said, "Amber's nascent fashion disaster—the first in an infinite line!"

Amber Salk is the t.b. (as in true-blue friend) in our crowd that Alanis totally named her album after, *Jagged Little Pill*. But like that ancient marinara poem we learned in eighth grade, she's our albatross. She hangs with us or on us. But without Ambu-tross in our lives, everything would be too perfect. And too much perfection would be boring. Like L.A. without mudslides or the absence of irregulars at the Calvin boutique. Amber's our annoying little ripple, disturbing the surface of a clear lake.

"I'm taking a boudoir break, Cher. Be right back," De announced as a commercial came on.

Personally? I like commercials and try not to miss them. Sometimes, they have way more wisdom than the shows they sponsor. Like that classic life-affirming one with Kate Moss for cK perfume that urged us to "Just Be." That is so massively deep. And I totally agree with it. It's almost like they created it with me in mind. Just being Cher Horowitz means just being an ordinary Beverly Hills Betty. Just being comes so naturally to me that I often "just be" on behalf of other people, too.

Take Daddy. It's been just the two of us since my mom died when I was a baby. Daddy's a heavy-duty attorney with a furious A-list of clients. Everyone he represents is either a CEO, CFO, COO, or a C-SPAN. It's way SRO. Daddy is so majorly bogged with work, he doesn't always take care of himself the way he should. That's where I come in. I coordinate his wardrobe, schedule appointments with his chiropractor, and fully supervise his monthly drive-bys with "those people." That's Daddy's pet name for his parents.

My special challenge is Daddy's diet. He is hugely nutritionally impaired. Some people say he's just plain huge. I try to sneak healthy but slimming whole grains and legumes onto the table at dinnertime. He tries to sneak whole candy bars and Twinkies under the table at every opportunity.

"But, Daddy, there's no actual food in that stuff. It's all chemicals," I tell him.

"There was a time, Cher," he always says, "when

better living through chemistry meant something in this world." That's when he usually swallows that last bit of faux chocolate.

All at once De was back on the line. It was like she'd read my mind. "It's awfully quiet on your end, Cher. Where's your dad tonight? Right about now, he's usually postal over something you tried to sneak into his dinner."

"Actually, De, I arranged for Daddy to be out tonight."

"Hello, Cher? Is there something you, like, forgot to tell me? Like maybe you've got a hottie coming over?"

Like maybe not. Tragically, De was wrong. "Not even." I sighed longingly, adding, "I sent Daddy to an important business dinner in the Valley."

De was shocked. Her voice went up about three decibels. I could barely hear the TV and Dylan's line to Brenda about how he didn't want to fall in love with her but couldn't help himself.

De was all "You sent your father to the Valley? Even if you had a fight with him, Cher, that's no way to get back at him. Besides, what business could he possibly have out there in Zappa land?"

De was referring to the San Fernando Valley, that blight on the landscape of Los Angeles that's fully barren in a cultural or, except for the Galleria, fashional sense. Although the Valley is only about twenty minutes from Beverly Hills—everything in L.A. is twenty minutes from everything else—it might as well be on planet Vacuum. De and I rarely venture there, but that is where I sent Daddy tonight.

"Tscha, De, this is business that's good for him. It's a Zone dinner seminar. It's for that important New Age breakthrough in weight reduction," I started to explain, but De already knew. When it comes to the cutting edge, whether it's diets, fashion, or aromatherapy, De prides herself on being ahead of the game. It's one of the myriad traits we have in common.

"The Zone," she was now saying, "as in that contra-carbo diet that's all hormonally correct?"

"You nailed it, girlfriend. It's all superhormones and eicosanoids. We all have good and bad ones," I said. I'd fully memorized the article I'd read in *Savvy* magazine's "In Shape" section. "The good ones help prevent disease, enhance your mental processes, improve your physical performance, and put you at the right body weight—hello? It puts you in the Zone. And the bad ones? Don't take me there. Anyway, Daddy needs to get into the Zone. I couldn't help it if the seminar was in the Valley."

"Righteous idea, Cher, but how did you get him to go?"

I paused before answering her, as the scene where Brenda and Dylan are about to fall into a zone of their own had started and I was riveted to the screen.

Then I explained how I'd convinced Daddy that he had to be at this meeting tonight. "I read him a powerful article—"

"The one in *Savvy*, about how forward-thinking the Zone is?"

"Not even. It was from an actual newspaper. The *L.A. Times*. It was an article about how one of the gurus on the Zone board of trustees might be sued for something and how he might need an important, forward-thinking lawyer."

"I so bow to your brilliance, Cher."

Just then on the big-screen TV the creases in Dylan's forehead deepened dramatically, and he leaned toward Brenda. They locked eyes. It was the most majorly intense moment of the entire first season. As I was savoring that historically nostalgic emotional high, I got a wholly unexpected icky feeling. Even though a parade of Baldwins had marched through my life, no one had ever looked at me exactly the way Dylan was looking at Brenda—not yet anyway. And I'm not impatient. I mean, I can so wait for gratification. Like when some designer original is about to go on sale, I never yield to temptation to buy it before markdown. But right at that second I felt as if I could not live another moment waiting for a love-struck studmuffin to gaze at me that way. I'm secure that will happen. I only wonder when.

I must have been wondering aloud, or De was demonstrating her powers of ESPN, because she said soothingly, "Don't worry, Cher, your hottie is out there."

"Like the truth?" I guessed.

"Just trust me, Cher. You'll know him when you see him."

"Is that how it was with you and Murray?" I asked, although I knew the answer. Murray was De's now and forever, the childhood crush that had morphed to true love. Only their love needed to hit a speed bump every once in a while to jog it back into gear. In school they're known as the Fighting Couple. They're way Bobby Brown and Whitney Houston, except Murray's never been to jail and De doesn't sing. Still, it's exactly the same.

Which reminded me. "By the way," I asked De, "it's

awfully quiet on your end, in a call-waiting sense. Where is Murray? Why is he not beeping you possessively? Isn't he supposed to be studying for that makeup test? And beeping you incessantly during his so-called study breaks?"

Due to an unforeseen delay—the Lakers game Murray attended went into overtime the night before—De's main had overslept and missed his first period English lit test. He was supposed to be studying for his makeup test tomorrow.

"He would be," De agreed, "only since he isn't at home studying, he isn't at home beeping. Murray's out with Sean. That theater in Westwood is showing a Jim Carrey-thon, and Dumb and Duh-head could not resist. It was like the father ship calling them home."

That Murray would be doing something typically boy zone, especially with his best bud-in-crime, Sean, wasn't surprising, but that he was doing it the night before his big makeup test was kind of unusual, even for him. Murray was naturally brilliant, and he thought our teachers should give him props for his natural abilities—whether or not he physically took a particular test. Our teachers did so not agree. Mr. Hall toyed with the idea of giving him an F, but Murray turned on the charm and Mr. Hall agreed to give him a makeup test. I had no doubt that Murray would ace it. I just thought he'd ace it better by cracking open the Cliff Notes.

I reached out and grabbed the angora throw from the end of the sectional and wrapped it tightly around myself. I leaned back. True love on the screen and my true blue on the other end of the line. Life was golden. It would be better, of course, if there was a significant

7

hottie on the couch next to me. Or even an interim insignificant.

I knew what was coming next. It was the big moment when Dylan and Brenda would lock lips for the first time. It was way passionate. I closed my eyes to fully absorb the emotional impact of it all. And that's when it happened.

"De! I can't believe it," I squealed. "The earth totally moved!"

There was no other way to explain the intensity of Dylan and Brenda's kiss. I felt the sectional separate. Call me mental, but even the Lladros on the mantle and Daddy's Litigator of the Year Award seemed to shake. First contact is that powerful, even if it's on a TV rerun.

De felt it, too. We are so in sync, as best friends should be. She was all "I'm there, Cher. It happened for me, too. I could feel that kiss!"

This time when the commercial came on, I had to get up. I was desperately in need of liquid infusion. I tossed off the angora throw and headed across the terra-cotta tiles into the kitchen. I surveyed the pickings in the fridge and considered calling out for a Starbucks mochaccino. Only forget what I said about waiting for gratification—I needed it instantly. I made do with freeze-dried, prebottled iced decaf latte and ambled back into the den.

When I got back, neither Dylan nor Brenda was on the screen. Nor was a commercial. Instead, it was some Jurassic news dude—like, how come the women on the news have to be babes while the men can be authentic fogies? I was about to discuss the rampant inequity of that with De, when I zoned in on what the news dude was droning on about.

". . . Early reports have it measuring a five point oh on the Richter scale. We don't yet know the extent of the damage, if any, but our NewsChopper Five crews are speeding to the scene." As I waited for him to say something about "and now we rejoin our show in progress," I noticed how his makeup was way uneven. Too much powder on one side, not enough on the other. I briefly considered calling the station to lend my makeup expertise. But then everything paled. It wasn't the announcer's foundation, it was his words. "To repeat, there has been a report of an earthquake in the Valley."

It was as if, like in that movie where Tom Cruise played the vampire, a stake went through my heart. It felt worse than getting a C-minus on a test, worse than the heartbreak of Saks being out of my Alaïa, worse than anything.

An earthquake in the Valley! How blond could I be? I thought the earth moved because Dylan kissed Brenda. The earth moved *because it really moved!* De thought so, too. What did that say about her?

Suddenly, I felt like I was in an echo chamber. I vaguely heard De whimpering about "Cher, did you hear that? The Galleria's in the Valley! What if it was hit? Tomorrow's the Chanel sale." Weakly she added, "Cher. Your father." De's voice trailed off. I dropped the phone. All I could think about was Daddy. All I could see was Daddy sliding off his chair, landing hard on the floor, and the Zone diet food and all its eicosanoids flying through the air. Superhormones crashing. I could hear Daddy yelling, "Cher! Cher! This is your fault! Why did I let you talk me into this? Never again will I listen to you!"

Daddy was *there*. And *there* was where the earthquake was. And he was there where the earthquake was all because of me.

Chapter 2

I had to get to Daddy.

I don't know exactly when or how, but apparently I managed to reach Josh in his college dorm. I don't know exactly when he came to get me. Time stood still, like when you're at a rock concert because you're into the lead singer, but the drum solo goes on interminably. Only I didn't check my Movado. I didn't even look for my Movado. I didn't even change my clothes. I bolted upstairs and slipped on my platform running shoes without caring if they even matched my sweats. I only know that sometime after that horrific news bulletin, the ex-stepbrother came crashing through the door. Josh was yelling something like, "Cher! Get that green stuff off your face!" Then he grabbed my hand and together we dashed out and jumped into his Jeep Laredo convertible.

"Did you try paging him, Cher?" Josh demanded as he screeched backward out the cobblestone driveway.

"Of course I did, you moron. There was no answer." I was a Betty on the verge. As I snapped the seat belt into place, I suddenly felt myself snap. I screamed, "We have to get to Daddy!"

I was way discombobulated. I'd even run out of the house without my cell phone, but I didn't care. I just kept repeating, "We have to save Daddy!" That must have scared Josh, who has never seen this side of me. Instead of being all "This is a hare-brained idea," and other bon mots from the usual collection of arguments that characterize our relationship, Josh was all "Be calm, Cher. I'm sure Mel is all right. Where did you say he was exactly?"

I managed to squeak out, "Sportsman's Lodge in Studio City."

"Hang on, Cher." Josh weaved in and out of lanes on Santa Monica Boulevard. "They probably closed off the canyons, so we'll take the freeway. We'll get there as soon as we can."

My hair, which is normally way Carolyn Bessette Kennedy, was totally tangling in the nighttime wind, but I didn't care. I would sacrifice anything for Daddy.

Josh reached out to flip on the radio, but I grabbed his hand. "No, don't," I beseeched. "I don't think I could bear it if the news is bad. Just drive, Josh. Hurry."

"You're being ridiculous, Cher," Josh said with a tinge of annoyance. "I had the news on all the way here, but the details were sketchy. They didn't even pinpoint where in the Valley it happened. It could be anywhere. Let's listen for updates." Again he attempted to punch the power button on.

"No! Josh, please. Don't put me through this. What I'm going through is hard enough." I felt that burning, upchucking sensation that comes when I've eaten a greasy chocolate croissant or that sappy Hallmark commercial is on.

Josh peered at me and his voice softened. "Don't cry, Cher. It's going to be all right."

"Cry! As if!" I sniffed. Crying is majorly not me. Crying in front of Josh could only mean one thing: the invasion of the wuss-snatchers has happened. I turned away and folded my arms across my chest, and we drove on in silence.

Then, just as Josh headed up the on-ramp of the freeway, we spoke at the exact same moment.

Anxiously I said, "What if the freeway is closed?"

Suspiciously he said, "What's Mel doing in the Valley anyway?"

Neither of us answered. Josh's silence gave him away. That, and the way his knuckles went an unflattering blue-veined white as he gripped the steering wheel. Even though Daddy was not Josh's biological parent, Josh felt this filial bond. Josh was scared, too, but not too scared to interpret my silence. The step-pain immediately suspected foul play, as in, Cher had something to do with Daddy's unusual whereabouts this evening.

"Maybe you didn't hear me," Josh yelled as he whisked into the left lane, totally cutting off a stretch limo. "I said, what's Mel doing in the Valley anyway?"

In my least defensive tone of voice I said, "He's at a seminar."

"Most of Mel's seminars, if they're even in town, are in Century City or at the Convention Center downtown. He didn't mention anything to me about one in the Valley. What was the topic?"

I pretended not to hear Josh.

"Answer me, Cher! What exactly is Mel doing in the Valley tonight?"

So much for pretending. Evenly, I just said, "I sent him there."

Josh gave me the look. He ought to have a patent on it. It's somewhere between shock and how could you be so stupid. "You sent Mel to the Valley. What hare-brained idea was this, Cher? Exactly what was so urgent?"

That's when I got defensive. And a little whiny. "It wasn't hare-brained, it was to get the toxins out."

I thought Josh's mouth was going to stay permed in the fruit-fly-catching position. Clearly, college boy was Zone-impaired. So, as we sped along the freeway, at the top of my lungs I tried to encapsulate the entire Zone concept as best I could. Since Josh was all hard-core political correctness, I ended with the way persuasive "It's about hormonal correctness."

Josh did not get it. Like, why am I surprised. He practically spat back at me, "Hormonal correctness! You are certifiable. I should use you in one of my psychology experiments. It's about being in on the fads, Cher, the trends, and that's *all* it's about. Wake up and smell the crackpots."

But Josh stopped short of full-tilt attack. Which was

worse than if he had barraged me with insults. I could practically hear him thinking, If something bad happened to Mel, it's Cher's fault.

How it could take this long to get to the Studio City exit? Formerly benign billboards took on ominous overtones. Like the ad for Must-See TV. What if Daddy never sees any TV again? Kramer was pointing the finger of guilt at me. When we passed the Claudia Schiffer milk mustache billboard, I made a sacred vow: if Daddy comes out of this all right, I promise to drink more milk. And help Lucy with my room.

Finally, I saw the sign for the exit. "Get off the freeway!" I screamed as Josh put the pedal to the metal and jumped three lanes. We were so close. I felt like I had cotton balls in my ears. I was sure there were sirens, ambulances, those high-tech, noisy newschopper things that hover around Madonna's house when she's getting married or having a baby. But I heard nothing. Way eerie silence. What if we were too late? I felt the freeze-dried latte on its way up.

And then we saw it. The Sportsman's Lodge, two terminally long blocks off the exit, was uh, the strangest thing. It was intact. Sprawling, low-slung, retro as ever: an *Architectural Digest* Don't.

"Are you thinking what I'm thinking, Cher?" Josh slowed the car to a crawl. His voice was laced with sarcasm. Which I ignored.

"What do you mean? Let's go find Daddy!"

"I mean, Cher, that there are no police, no ambulances, no rubble, no news crews. There's clearly no earthquake here." Josh's voice had, like, gone up the scales and was in major decibels. He practically shouted, "And maybe if you'd let me turn on the radio, we would have known that."

I matched him shout for shout. "I don't care. Pull into the parking lot. I'm going to find Daddy anyway." Okay, so a part of me knew I was being, like, a total bonehead. But I couldn't shake the feeling that I'd come close to losing Daddy, and if I had, it would have been all my fault. Now that we were here, I had to make sure he was all right. Even if all the evidence pointed to exactly that.

Josh rolled his eyes, turned into the parking lot, and glided into a spot. He was way exasperated. "I don't get you, Cher. I just don't."

"I'm going to find Daddy. You can come with me or not. Whatever." With that, I bolted toward the entrance. In a flash Josh was right beside me. "You know what, Cher? You're about to make a giant fool of yourself, and I wouldn't miss this for the world."

Completely ignoring the step-drone's diss, I strode purposefully into the main lobby. It screamed decorator distress. According to the cheesy electronic sign, the Grabowitz bar mitzvah was in Ballroom A, some dental floss convention was in Ballroom B, and the Zone seminar in Ballroom C. I swung through the double doors and was immediately enveloped in a sea of Zone believers.

Furtively, I scanned for Daddy. As I elbowed my way through the room, I realized that conversations were coming to abrupt halts as gauntlets of Zone-heads stopped to rudely stare at me and Josh. I couldn't figure out why, until I suddenly realized what we were wearing. Amid this sea of pin-striped suits and designer ensembles, we were woefully underdressed, me in my *Flashdance* sweats, Josh in his ragged jeans and crumpled T-shirt. It was like, if we were Waldo, no one would have trouble spotting us.

Suddenly, a smooth ancestral type was at my side. "Can I help you?" he asked, all faux sincere. I could practically see the little bubble over his head that said, "I'm calling security."

If I'd had heels, which tragically I didn't, I would have dug them in. So I thrust out my chin and stood my ground. "I'm here to find——" But I didn't get the words out. All at once I heard the rumbling. It was the sweetest sound in the world: Daddy. I felt his paternal aura surround me as he thundered, "Cher! Josh! What's wrong? Are you all right?"

"Daddy! Daddy!" I whirled and threw my arms around him. "I kept seeing you falling off your chair . . . and blaming me!" I knew I was babbling nonsensically, but that's what happens when you're massively relieved, as I was—not only that Daddy was okay, but that he'd taken my advice and worn the Prada suit. It was totally the way to go here.

We were making a major scene, so Daddy put his arm around me and said, "Let's discuss this outside." He led us out of the ballroom. Kids from the Grabowitz bar mitzvah in funky hats and oversize sunglasses were running through the lobby.

Daddy was all "What is this all about? What are the two of you doing here?"

Josh opened his mouth to speak, but I jumped in. "We heard about the earthquake. Didn't you even feel it?"

"What earthquake? You mean that little quiver

about an hour ago? Sure, we all felt a slight rumble, and a few glasses of water got knocked over, but it was so minor we figured it was out in Pasadena or something. Someone at my table flipped on a compact TV. Turns out it was centered in Agoura Hills, but just a four point five. No major damage, and no one was hurt." Daddy peered at me suspiciously. "What exactly did you kids hear?"

This time Josh turned to me. He folded his arms across his chest. "I think I'll let Cher explain that, Mel."

Since I didn't want to admit my oops, I sputtered, "But, Daddy, I tried calling you. Why didn't you answer the page?"

Daddy looked blank for a second. Then it hit him. "Oh, no. When the meeting began, so many phones and pagers were ringing, they asked everyone to turn them off so the speaker could be heard. I must have gotten distracted and forgotten to turn mine back on. I corralled Decker, the client I've been trying to land, and I was just about to make my pitch when you two burst in."

My eyes were downcast. The carpet needed upgrading. "I'm sorry, Daddy. I didn't mean . . . I just thought you were in the earthquake and . . ."

Daddy didn't go ballistic, but he *was* heading toward rankled. "Look, kids, go home. As you can see, everything's fine. I'm going back to Decker." Just then I noticed a Milky Way sticking out of Daddy's jacket pocket. Surreptitiously, I slipped it out. "I know you'll nail him, but I think you'll have a better shot without this."

Daddy got all faux gruff. "Just go home, Cher." He looked over at Josh. "I'm sure you two thought there was some real catastrophe, but as you can see, there isn't. But there will be if you stay, so shoo! Both of you, leave." With that, Daddy gave me a giant hug. I hugged him back, then wiped off his jacket where I made the smudge with what was left of my herbal mask.

Josh was all Mr. Stony Silence as we walked back to the car. He didn't say a word until we turned onto the freeway, and then he was megasarcastic. "Is it okay if I turn the radio on now, Cher?"

"Whatever."

The reports on the radio clearly detailed a minor 4.5 shake several towns away in the San Fernando Valley. I went for lighthearted. "Isn't that just like L.A., to overestimate the number on the Richter scale just like they overestimate the grosses on movies?"

Josh took that as his cue to attack me. "And isn't that just like you to jump to conclusions without waiting to find out the details."

"Excuse me. I was worried about Daddy, so maybe I overreacted a little."

"A little? Cher, you practically had me believing the worst."

I shuddered. "Well, anyway, everything's okay, Daddy's fine and nobody was hurt anywhere. I need to call De. She's probably into major palpitations. Where's your cell phone?" I looked around the Jeep but didn't see one, so I opened the glove compartment. The only thing that tumbled out was a book, or two books in one, a spiritual tome on Zen and some repair manual, *The Art of Motorcycle Maintenance*. Since Josh didn't have a motorcycle, I couldn't figure what he'd be doing with that.

"You can stop hunting, Cher. I don't have a cellular phone in the car. I know this may come as a huge shock, but not everyone does. Only to sheltered little Beverly Hills princesses is the cellular phone a necessity."

I was stung. "That was harsh, Josh. Why are you on planet Grumpy anyway?"

"Why am I *what?* You almost had me believing something terrible happened to Mel—all because you wouldn't wait and listen, and worse, you wouldn't let *me* wait and listen. Now you expect me to just turn around and be lighthearted? I'm not as superficial as you are. I can't just turn my emotions on and off like a faucet."

"Superficial! As if! Excuse me, your deepness, but what's the big deal anyway? We took a little ride, saw Daddy was okay. Besides, what were you doing that was so important you couldn't interrupt it?"

"I was watching *Jeopardy!* if you must know."

"Oh, well. That explains your pique. Call me mental, but isn't *Jeopardy!* the nerd-alert game show you tried out for and didn't get on? You know, Josh, you've really got to work on that masochistic streak of yours. I know several excellent therapists."

"I don't think so, Cher. See, I wasn't watching alone, if you get my drift. And Melanie, who *did* get on, was with me. We were watching the College Tournament together, seeing her trample the competition."

Josh bagged a Betty? I don't know why, but I suddenly felt icky all over again. The rampant need to call De overtook me.

"Whatever, Josh. I still don't see what any of that has

to do with you not having a mobile phone. Everyone has one. I bet even your brainiac girlfriend does."

"No, she doesn't—and who said she was my girlfriend? You have the most annoying way of getting off topic."

"I didn't know we were on topic."

"I'll speak slowly then. Our topic was you and the fact that you are so sheltered you have absolutely no concept of reality." Josh was all smug. And I was buggin'.

"As if! I am way reality-centric."

Josh harrumphed. "In your world, maybe—a world without have-nots, a world where trees are slashed and burned to make room for parking lots, where all the problems of humanity are obscured beneath a shiny patina of designer fashions and luxury cars."

"Your point?" I bristled. "And what does that restaurant on Melrose called Patina have to do with it?"

"Your honor, I rest my case." Josh swung off the freeway and hit the brakes at the light by Wilshire.

"Josh, I have no idea what you're talking about. I think the near trauma of the last half hour has seized your brain cells. There is nothing wrong or obscure about my world. Maybe it is shiny, but just in case you hadn't heard, shiny is in now. Anyway, that doesn't make it any less real."

"It's not the real world, Cher."

"Excuse me, is this the part where you tell me Puck was the only authentic character in *The Real World?*"

Josh totally rolled his eyes. "Let's put it this way. You, Cher Horowitz, could never survive in the real world. You could not make it one month without Mel's largesse."

"Hello? Daddy's largesse is exactly what I was trying to get under control with the Zone. Didn't you even hear anything I was saying before?"

Josh had that same exasperated tone in his voice that Daddy had had a little while before. "Largesse—as in Mel's credit cards and his generous personality, not his largeness."

"Excuse me," I reminded Josh. "I don't see you exactly deprived of Daddy's large-whatevers. As in, where did this Jeep come from? Just because you don't have a cell phone, that makes you so much more worthy than I am?"

"Low blow, Cher. You know I intend to pay Mel back for the wheels as soon as I can."

"Whatever. So, what else, in your *vast* experience, do 'real world' people do that I don't?"

"Okay, I'll give you that. I have had certain luxuries in my life, but at least I'm in touch with reality. I know most people don't have mobile phones, certainly don't have limitless access to credit cards. They don't have cable TV. Even at your age, a lot of people have jobs because they need the money."

"They do so have cable TV!" I was pretty sure of that one.

But Josh acted as if I'd proved his point. "See, that's what I mean. You have no concept at all. Without the protection of your gilded Beverly Hills existence, you'd be completely lost."

"As if I I would not be lost. Daddy says I am way directionally enhanced. I am totally equipped to deal with any world. Gilded or matte. Whatever."

"Really." Josh had this new tone in his voice. Know-it-all mixed with bemused. "Okay, Cher, you think so?

Prove it. I bet you can't make it thirty days without your credit cards, without your cell phone. Let's go all the way here. Let's see if you can get and keep a paying job—for a period of one month."

Live without my cell phone? Without my credit cards? What did the step-drone think that would prove? And as for a job? What did Josh call taking care of Daddy and keeping up my *über*-popular status? But somehow I knew he wouldn't recognize the worthiness of all that. I wondered if Mela-tonin, or whatever his girlfriend's name was, had a job.

For the second time that night I stuck out my chin. "You know what? You are so on, Josh. I hereby accept your challenge—with a few caveats." I was way proud of myself. I used to think caveats went best with crackers, but now I know it means conditions.

"Name them." Josh pulled into our driveway and turned off the motor. He faced me full on. I almost got off point again wondering if he looked at Mela-brain with the same intensity in his baby blues.

"Okay, this is a bet. So if I win—which, hello! I will—here's what you, the loser, have to do."

"Go ahead, Cher. I'm listening."

I had to think fast, because it's not as if I'd planned on making a bet with Josh tonight. I flipped my mental remote through all the channels, trying to come up with something. Then I suddenly flashed on Dylan and Brenda and that kiss. Lightbulb!

"Okay, so when I win our bet, you, Josh, will introduce me to *three* hotties you know from college."

Josh put his hands up and started to interrupt. "Oh, no, Cher, that's not what this is about."

"Well, it's a bet isn't it?" I said, batting my bare

eyelashes and doing coy as best I could under the circumstances. "And since you're going to lose—and personally, I don't think I have to prove anything to you—there has to be a payoff for me. This is what I want: college Baldwins. Three, because I want a selection."

"What's the matter, Cher, is there no selection left on the smorgasbord of boys at your school?" For the first time that night, Josh had his familiar teasing tone back.

He was right, though. Boys my age are like the human equivalent of comic books. I was ready for classic drama. Like Danielle Steel.

"Okay, Cher. I accept."

"You do?"

"Sure. Since you're not going to win, it's a moot point anyway. Now we get to the part where I say what I win when you're forced to admit that I was right— you can't cope in the real world."

"Whatever, Josh."

"I would have been happy just to have the satisfaction of proving you wrong, but since you upped the stakes, I'm game. When I win, you will be part of my psych experiment. I'm taking abnormal psychology, and one of my labs is to measure the brain waves of two volunteer students."

Me? A brain-wave Mother Teresa? Like that is ever going to happen. "Knock-knock: anybody home? This is me, Josh. Cher Horowitz. And I'm not going to lose."

As I jumped out of the car and dashed toward my front door, I heard Josh calling, "Just to show you what a nice guy I am, I'll give you a week to get ready. Ditch the credit cards, fold the phone, and get a job. Should be a snap, right? After all, you're Cher Horo—"

I was inside our domed foyer before he got the "witz" out.

Chapter 3

*P*roject! Nothing inspires me more than a challenge—except, of course, the Paris fashion shows. I drove to school the next day, a Betty on a mission. Unlike the mission in that classic Tom Cruise movie, mine was possible and easy to comprehend. First, I needed an emergency caucus with my t.b.'s to bring them up to speed on last night's titanic events and enlist their help in my already formulating plan. We were meeting just before homeroom.

I go to Bronson Alcott High School, which is the public school in our district. I swung into my reserved spot in Parking Lot B and was just about to alight, when I heard someone call out, "One spot to a customer, Cher. Move your car." It was Brian Fuller, our anal-retentive class president, whose parking spot was next to mine. So what if I'd inched into his vehicular territory a teensy bit? Like, who painted those lines so close together anyway? I climbed back in the Jeep and did a vehicular redial.

"Cher!" I turned toward the sound of De's voice. She was bounding toward me as fast as her five-inch Joan & David's could take her. "I'm massively relieved your father's all right." De knew before I did that Daddy wasn't even near the real earthquake, but she totally felt my pain anyway.

"Fully operational," I agreed, returning her t.b. hug.

Along our school's muraled walls and all down the polished linoleum corridors, De and I rule as the most envied Bettys in the entire sophomore class. As natural leaders, it's our duty to spread style and inspiration wherever we go. We bring hope to the hopelessly fashion-impaired, style sense to the senseless. That's why we never take our school outfits lightly. Today, for instance, I'd chosen the diagonally striped BCBG Max Azria dress with the Steve Madden chunky platforms I'd snared on sale this week. De had done her stretchy flat-front flare Dollhouse hip-huggers and midriff-baring crop-top.

"Hola, amigas." I detached myself from De and came face-to-vainglorious-face with Amber. Tragically, I had to include her in the caucus, as I would need a plethora of assists to win my bet with Josh. Fashion victim Amber was all jungle-patterned tights and spotted Dalmatian dress. Like, hello? Animal prints are so last semester! I would have hit the mute button about her fashion flop du jour, but Amber was all "I heard you made a fool of yourself breaking and entering some business dinner last night. Way to go, Cher."

27

What? Had my major oops made the ten o'clock news?

De connected the dots. "Amber's uncle was there."

I rebounded quickly. "Whatever. At least I'm not making a fool of myself in an outdated get-up like that. When they say retro, they still mean this millennium, Amber."

Amber ignored my diss, as the three of us headed into the Quad, the terraced inner courtyard thoughtfully provided for student relaxation and nutrition breaks. As our peer-group populace hurried by us into the ivy-covered building, De, Amber, and I perched on the marble benches while I recounted last night's events, ending with the no-credit-card, ban-on-cellphone, job-snagging challenge issued by Josh.

At first neither of my girlfriends was fully supportive.

"I can't believe you took that bet with Josh." De was way amazed. "What do you care what the step-burden thinks anyway?"

"Why would you put yourself in such a compromising position?" Amber added.

"While I totally bow to your expertise in compromising positions, Amber, this one is in the bag. I already have a foolproof plan."

De narrowed her sharp, exquisitely made-up hazel eyes at me. "Describe."

So I did. At breakfast, while Daddy was lecturing me about never again attempting to go near an earthquake site—even if, hello, there was no earthquake—I formulated a brilliant, highly conceptualized design scheme.

"Okay, so for a month, I can't use my credit cards."

De and Amber shuddered involuntarily.

"But, girlfriends, *you* can use yours."

Way off track as usual, Amber gloated. "So we'll be at the mall while you're slaving away at some rinky-dink job thing?"

Not even. De got it immediately. "Wake up, Amber. Cher will simply put her charges on our cards, and after a month goes by, she'll pay us back." De was filled with admiration. "Chronic, Cher. The bills won't even be in by then."

Amber, who refused to give me snaps, was all "And the self-imposed drought on your cell phone usage? Exactly how do you intend to shoulder the unthinkable burden of that?"

"Okay, I admit that will be more of a challenge, but it's basically the same concept."

"You want *us* to make your calls for you?" Amber was horrified. Reflexively, she reached into her Tig-nanello backpack and protectively cradled her mobile.

But once again De was all there. "Tscha, Amber, this is war. It may not be a battle you or I would have chosen, but we will fully enlist for Cher. It's the only noble thing to do. Besides, it's for a limited time only."

Grudgingly, Amber participated in our traditional, patented limp-wristed high five.

Now only the last part of the equation was left to solve: the job thing. To do that, like the person in that famous poem, I had to veer off to a road not taken, a road that led to the guidance office where, I was told, something called job postings could be found. Before we headed off to first period, we all agreed to meet at the guidance office during lunch. Naturally, Amber had to have the last word. "I hope you appreciate what I'm giving up for you."

While I thought she'd be better off giving up her George-of-the-jungle leggings, her words were not without merit. Since my t.b.'s *had* graciously given up prime Quad-viewing time to help me search out employment opportunities, I did what any grateful friend would do: I catered. Using my cell phone for what would be close to the last time for a month, I called out to Spago, the furiously famous gourmet pizza parlor on Sunset. I ordered enough for Miss Geist, our social studies teacher, who's also our guidance counselor.

"This was very thoughtful of you, Cher," Geist said as a dollop of pizza sauce escaped down her chin and settled onto her blouse. There, it formed one of those Horshack test patterns. It reminded me of Josh and his psych experiment. Quickly, I dipped my Hermes handkerchief into my Evian water and gave it to her. "Here, Miss Geist. If you blot gently at it, the dry cleaners have a better shot at getting it out."

Geist was rampantly grateful. When she finished her last slice, she got up and gingerly removed a thick folder from the shelf above her desk. It was labeled Student Job Opportunities/Community Service. She dusted it off and handed it to me.

"Here you go, Cher. Take your time. There are a lot of listings. Not many students here at Bronson Alcott take advantage of this service. I'm glad to see you leading the way. Maybe more students will follow." She smiled hopefully.

I wanted to explain to Geist that this wasn't part of

my leadership duties, but I didn't have it in me to dash that look of optimism on her face. So I just nodded and took the folder from her. As I plunked it down on the desk, De and Amber pulled up chairs on either side of me. The folder was stuffed with sheets of paper, each describing a job or volunteer position. I hoped there was something quick and painless: a troika of college hotties awaited.

"'Dairy Queen needs part-timer for scooping and serving,'" De read from the top sheet. "'Will train in Slush preparation.'" While those were worthy skills, I felt pretty sure I was more DKNY than DQ. We turned to the next page.

"'Friendly's has openings for waitress trainees,'" Amber read, taunting, "I can just see you in a frilly little apron with a Cher name tag. 'May I tell you what our specials are today?'"

"Point taken, Amber," De reprimanded. Just then her beeper went off. "It's Murray," she said, ignoring it. "I'll call him back later. Let's continue." De flipped to the next page. Her eyes were riveted to the top, where the words Chanel Boutique were printed. I picked it up and read, "'Unique opportunity for highly qualified student . . .'" The words "boutique," "unique," and "highly qualified" all in one sentence were a promising beginning. It continued, "'. . . to fill one trainee slot still open in our sales force.'"

"Do it! Take it! This is the one!" Amber leaped out of her seat and was into over-the-top squeals. She reminded me of Babe. I wondered why Amber was so drastically psyched. I didn't have to wonder long. "You'll get a huge discount! We'll all get huge discounts! Where's the number? Here, use my cell phone. Call them up now and tell them you'll take it!"

I was about to when my finger froze on the power button. A vision suddenly materialized. There I was, perfectly put together in a cute little Chanel ensemble, handing over a severely chic number to a customer—who looked a lot like Amber. It *was* Amber! If I took this position it would mean I'd have to wait on Amber, who would never let me or our entire school forget the heinous humiliation of me serving her. I could not take myself there.

"You know what, Amber?" I said, handing her back the phone. "I think not. I'm going to keep looking."

"What are you saving yourself for, Cher? You think Armani's got a listing in here? Don't let this one slip away. It's got your name written all over it."

De held up the next posting. "This might work, Cher. The MAC makeup counter at Bloomingdale's needs someone experienced to do makeovers on random customers."

I considered. "An important service to humanity, but would that not involve standing for hours in my platforms? It could be dangerous to my arches. It seems an unnecessary health risk."

De nodded sagely. "You're right. What was I thinking?"

"How about this, Cher?" Amber waved the next sheet in my face, "Domino's Driver. Now that you finally have your license, I think you'd be the perfect pizza delivery babe, no?"

Amber was still gloating because she'd snared her driver's license before the rest of us. She's way skilled at holding a gloat.

"Actually, Amber," I countered, "since you're the more experienced driver, I'll unselfishly step aside to make room for you on this one. Why not take it?"

"I *am* more experienced, Cher, but may I remind you, moi is not the one who *needs* a job. That would be you."

Just at that moment, the door to the guidance office burst open, banging against the wall. We all spun around. It was Murray, quickly followed by Sean. I wondered what was up with Sean's hair: I knew he was growing it out. I didn't know he was planning on dyeing it rust. I didn't get a chance to ask why, because Murray was going off on De. "There you are! I have been looking all over for you, woman! Why have you not answered my page?" Before De could respond, Murray was all "This is an emergency! I need you! I am in the middle of a life-threatening, scare-tactic, earth-shaking crisis!"

De was unmoved. "Take a number."

"What's up with you, woman? Did you not hear me?"

"The whole zip code heard you, Murray, only yours isn't the only crisis I'm dealing with. Cher's crisis came first."

"What's up with Cher?" Sean asked, genuinely curious. He sidled up to me. That's when I noticed the earring. It too was new.

Amber answered him. "Cher needs a job."

Murray put his own travails on hold. His eyes widened. "You having financial problems?"

"As if!" De answered for me and then explained my predicament, including the part about my having to be in Josh's experiment if I lost the bet.

33

Murray rolled his eyes. "You women! That ain't crisis material. I got the real deal, here."

Sean saw the picture more clearly. "We gotta save Cher from bein' a lab rat in some psycho experiment."

I turned to Sean. "Thanks for understanding. What's with the new image?"

Murray was not about to be derailed. "Forget him. He just bought the Dennis Rodman Starter Kit and he's trying it out. We gotta concentrate on *my* problem."

I closed the folder. It didn't look like the temporary job of my dreams was hiding inside anyway. I regarded Murray, who looked as discombobulated as I had last night. One of the earflaps on his Kangol hat was sticking straight up, while the other remained locked in the down position. "What's the matter, Murray? Did you fail the makeup test?" I guessed.

"Worse."

"What's worse than getting an F on a makeup test Hall was considerate enough to give you to atone for the F you got for missing the original test?"

"Expulsion."

The word sent shock waves around the room. It was like the earthquake last night, only without the kiss. No one spoke. Shakily, De got up from her chair and walked over to Murray. She took his hand and looked up into his eyes, where actual fear lurked. Softly De said, "Sit down, baby. Tell me. We'll fix it."

I was beyond flipped. "You're getting expelled for whiffing on a test? Isn't your father, like, a major school benefactor?"

"It's not the school," Murray said gravely. "It *is* my father."

De's hand flew up to her mouth. Murray's dad defined no nonsense. "How did he find out you failed? Didn't you just take it this morning?"

"He called the school. But it's more than that. From the minute I walked in last night from the Jim Carreython, he's been in my business. He's like 'This is twice this week you been out on a school night! I'm calling the principal to find out what's going on there.'"

"What did Principal Lehman say?" I asked.

"He just said, you know, the usual: that I don't pay attention, I'm not workin' up to potential, blah, blah, blah."

Amber was all "But that's what school authorities always say. What's the big deal?"

"The big deal," Murray said, his eyes downcast, "is that my father took it seriously. He just beeped me and said"—Murray lowered his voice in an imitation of his father—"'Son, your mother and I are not happy with the way things are progressing here. This school is far too lenient. If we don't take steps now, you won't get into an Ivy League college.'"

Then Murray cupped De's face in his hands, looked deeply into her eyes, and said, "Baby, he wants me to transfer to a private school. He wants me out of here— far away, to a military school in another state. He's calling for applications as we speak."

No one said a word. I looked at De. She was shaking. A tear was forming in the corner of her left eye. I ran to Miss Geist and retrieved my handkerchief. No sense in De ruining her makeup.

Miss Geist spoke first. "Isn't there anything we can do, Murray? Anything to get your father to reconsider?"

Murray was too overcome with emotion to respond. He and De hugged some more, and then all of us, even Amber, formed a giant hug circle around the two of them and held on tightly. Murray leaving school? Callously ripped away from life as he knows it, slashed apart from us and from De? This was beyond catastrophic. It was a travesty.

A reserve of strength I didn't know I had suddenly overtook me. I had to do something to stop this heinous turn of events before any more damage was inflicted. I heard myself saying with major conviction, "Don't worry, Murray. We will think of something. We will *not* let you leave us."

Everyone turned to look at me hopefully.

Sean seconded. "What she said."

And now there were two—projects, that is: finding a job and finding a way to keep Murray among the living well, that is, us. It weighed heavily on me as I returned home that afternoon. As I approached the grand staircase that leads up to my room, I heard Daddy bellowing from his study.

"Is that you, Cher?"

The sound of his voice was uplifting. I decided to seek his advice and swung into his study. Daddy was standing in front of his mahogany desk, sorting through some papers. His glasses were on top of his head.

I came around and gave him a peck on the cheek.

"What's that for?" he asked, in his faux-gruff way.

"I'm just glad you're all right, Daddy."

"I was never in any danger, Cher. You know that."

"Still, can't I just be grateful?"

Daddy looked up from his papers and regarded me quizzically. "What's going on, Cher? Did something happen in school today?"

Opting for minimalist, I said, "I need a job, Daddy."

"No, you don't, Cher. School is your job." Daddy went back to his papers.

Something told me that Daddy would not see the up side of my bet with Josh, especially the payoff-when-I-win part. Daddy's protective parental vibe kicks into overdrive if I merely mention boys and dating. The concept of me being introduced to college boys is enough to rocket him to nuclear city.

Thinking on my feet—even when I'm in chunky platforms—is one of my natural strengths, and I summoned it now. I recalled a conversation I'd had with Daddy in this very room not long ago. It was when I was trying to convince him of the worthiness of allowing me to star in an exercise video for teenagers. Okay, so in the end it didn't work out, but I do remember a soupçon of our interface.

"Daddy? Remember when you said, and I quote, 'Cher, if you want an after-school job, I can arrange one for you'?"

Daddy was all "I said that?" Then he got all suspicious. "Is there a boy involved in this sudden decision, Cher? Or did you max out your credit cards and are afraid to tell me?"

"Tscha, Daddy. It's nothing like that." I wasn't lying

about the boy part, because, doy, who considers Josh a boy? As for the college Baldwins waiting to meet me, well, that would happen later, so it didn't technically count now. "I just want to expand my horizons, you know, dabble in . . . the real world a little." I could not believe I was practically quoting Josh! Still, it seemed to have some effect on Daddy, who sat down and clasped his hands together on his desk and regarded me carefully.

"Just what kind of an after-school job did you have in mind, Cher? There's plenty of work around here."

I didn't think Josh would count working for Daddy, so I sped on. "I just want something, you know, different. Where I could be in a fresh environment, meet new people. I even looked through all the job postings at school, but there was nothing remotely right for me."

Daddy was significantly impressed. "You're really serious about this, aren't you? How come you never mentioned it before?"

I considered. Then I came up with the way convincing and partially true "Last night's mock trauma really got me thinking, Daddy. It shook me up. I don't know, it just made me see how much life has to offer, and I want to taste all of it." That last bit almost threw Daddy off the hook, but then he shrugged his ample shoulders, slid his glasses down onto his nose, and said, "Hand me my Rolodex. I'll make a call."

"You will?"

As Daddy flipped through the cards in his phone file, he mused, "I was just talking to Norman Goldberg, my accountant. I'm pretty sure he mentioned his nephew was just put in charge of some magazine. The only reason it stuck with me is because I've seen it in the pile on your floor. Don't you subscribe to J. Crew or something?"

"J. Crew is a catalogue, Daddy," I corrected him gently, "like Victoria's Secret, but with more layers." I wondered which magazine Daddy's accountant's nephew was boss of.

I was feeling way optimistic as Daddy punched in the number. A job at a magazine, depending on which one, could be furiously dope.

On the phone Daddy was saying, "That's terrific, Norman. Wait, let me write down the address." He turned to me. "Cher, grab a pen, write this down."

I fished one of my pink feather-tipped number two pencils out of my backpack and wrote as Daddy dictated, "*Savvy* magazine, 2040 Wilshire Boulevard, Suite 304. Yeah, she'll be there next Tuesday after school. Thanks again, Norm. Yeah, appreciate it. Talk to you tomorrow."

When Daddy hung up, he said, "You know this publication, right?"

Savvy magazine? Hello! That was only the most chronic teen magazine around. It featured the most golden fashions, life-altering advice columns, mind-bending quizzes, and the cream of celebrity Baldwin interviews. Not only have I heard of it, I'm fully committed to it. And now I'm going to be working there? I could not wait to tell De!

Daddy was explaining. "Norman says they run some kind of internship program. It's for high school kids only. You work a few days after school, they pay minimum wage, but they teach you all about publishing. The program was technically closed—in fact, it already started. Ordinarily, highly qualified kids apply months ahead of time for this, but Norman owed me one, so he's pulling some strings to get you in. I hope you're happy with this."

"Oh, Daddy, I am beyond happy. I am approaching Rosie O'Donnell when Tom Cruise went on her show! Thank you, thank you, thank you, Daddy. You are so prime! I have to call De!"

I bounded upstairs, did a belly flop onto my bed, and reached for the phone. I was just about to speed dial De when I had a better idea. I punched in Josh's dorm digits.

"Hey, Freud, guess what?" I said teasingly when he answered. "Better find some other porker for your psych experiment, 'cause this babe just got a job."

If Josh was impressed, which he should have been, he didn't let it slip. Instead, he was all "You got Mel to pull some strings for you already?"

I could not believe Josh figured it out so fast! "How I got the job is not your concern," I bristled, "but be warned. I start on Tuesday after school. So start your search engine: you have thirty days to find me a trio of acceptable college Baldwins and a replacement for me in your psychology experiment." Then I added playfully, "Maybe Melanie wants to take my place."

"Overconfidence does not become you, Cher. Just because Mel finagled you a job doesn't mean you've won our bet. There was a lot more to it, if you remember. No cellular phone, no credit cards, and you have to keep the job, not just sashay in for a day."

"Whatever, Josh. I know what the bet was, and I'm

40

prepared to honor it fully. So, hello, it's like, watch out real world, here I come!"

Josh laughed. "I don't know if the real world could ever be prepared for you, Cher, but if you say you're ready, then I'm ready. We start Tuesday."

"I can't wait," I teased. Just then I heard a familiar TV theme song in the background on Josh's end. I flashed on Josh and his mentally enhanced Monet scanning the tube together. "Did I interrupt something?" I asked coyly.

"I was watching *Jeopardy!* You should try it. Exercise your brain cells for a change instead of just swinging shopping bags."

It didn't surprise me that Josh failed to appreciate the aerobic workout swinging heavy shopping bags provides. So I just said, "My brain cells are fine, Josh. I'm smart enough to outwit you, aren't I?" I was about to continue on my favorite express train of thought, sparring with Josh, when my I felt my brain cells actually stir. They were furiously swirling. An idea was forming, and it was stellar. "Joshie," I said sweetly, "don't hang up, yet. I need to ask you something."

He must've been stunned, because in all our years of step-rivalry, I have never resorted to a gushy pet name. But I couldn't help myself. I needed something from him, and it was radically unselfish. It was for Murray.

It suddenly hit me that, what if Murray got on *Jeopardy!?* Didn't they have that Teen Tournament thing? And Murray is such a whiz, he's bound to ace it. And if he did, wouldn't that prove to his father how much he's really absorbed at Bronson Alcott

High School? Murray's dad would see that he belonged in public school. With us. It was brilliant! It was . . . me!

Josh was saying, "What is it, Cher? Why are you calling me that?"

"Joshie, didn't you try out for like *Jeopardy! Jr.* or something?"

"Last year. Their Teen Tournament. You know I did. So?"

"So talk to me about it. Tell me the whole, full process. I'm *massively* interested."

Chapter 4

*U*sually, my weekends are all On your mark, get set, shop! Then segue. Get set, get dressed, party! But due to the unforeseen events of the past two days, a whole new agenda had leapfrogged to the head of the priority list. I had to convince Murray that *Jeopardy!* was the answer. The question: What is the most excellent way to get Murray to stay in school? So I called an emergency Saturday morning brunch caucus. Lucy whipped up the phone and called Barney Greengrass for a pastiche of trendy brunchtime foods like sushi and mini bagels.

De was first to arrive. I had to give her snaps for her just-thrown-together-yet-amazingly-appropriate Saturday A.M. attire: Dolce & Gabbana brocade pants under a matching calf-brushing gold brocade jacket.

Murray and Sean, the gruesome twosome, bounded

in soon after. On the up side, Sean had rinsed the rust out of his hair. On the down side, he'd obviously spent Friday night at Tattoo-U, as a finely detailed Chicago Bulls logo now decorated his left bicep. Sean assured me it was totally temporary yet necessary for step two of the Dennis Rodman Starter Kit.

Amber flounced in fashionably late. That was the only thing fashionable about Ambu-laminate. She seemed to be vying for the title of Ms. Plastic Fantastic, judging by her shocking pink shiny vinyl outfit. As she slipped a mini bagel and lox ensemble onto her plate, she whined, "I hope you appreciate the sacrifice I've made, Cher. To be here this morning, I had to reschedule my trainer, move my tennis lesson to the afternoon, and bump my shiatsu massage to next week."

"While I applaud your efforts at self-improvement, Amber, even you have to agree that Murray's grave situation takes priority. Which is why we're all here. We're wholly sacrificial, like that famous anthem, 'Keep smiling, keep shining'—a part you obviously took literally—'that's what friends are for.'"

De and Murray, huddled on the end of the sectional, took a break from feeding each other little bits of sushi to nod in agreement.

"Okay, so, thank you all for coming," I began. "While some of you were otherwise occupied last night"—I shot Sean a look—"I took action." Then I explained my idea of Murray's going on *Jeopardy!* to prove to his dad how much he'd learned at Bronson Alcott High School. I was ready to accept deserved applause from my t.b.'s, but instead I got major skepticism.

Murray stood up and started pacing the room. "I don't know, Cher. I mean, thanks for trying, but I've seen that show. I got it goin' on upstairs and all, but I ain't no superbrain, nerd-patrol friend of Steven Hawking's."

Then Sean stood up. "What he said."

Then I stood up. "Murray! Sean! Hello! *Jeopardy!*'s not just for card-carrying members of Club Mensa. It's *trivia!*"

Then, unfortunately, Amber stood up and deadpanned, "And excuse me. Who's more trivial than you, Murray? Well, maybe Sean." She was all squeaking vinyl as she sashayed over to the juice bar.

Then De leaped up and crossed the room. She stopped short of landing directly in Amber's face. "Oh, excuse *me*. I thought I heard something, but it was just some Ambu-mosquito with a death wish."

Amber took a swill of orange juice and did faux exasperated. "Look, Dionne, far be it from me to want to see Murray transferred, but I have to be honest. Murray's only chance at winning on *Jeopardy!* is if the categories are Jim Carrey movies and greasy foods."

"Don't diss my man, Amber. He's an intellectual," De growled.

Murray walked over and put a Hilfigered arm around De. "I don't know, De. Even if my old man buys it, I'm not sure I'm up to this."

Sean must have thought he was at a cheerleading rally, because he started pumping the air and going, "Yes, we can! We can do this, bro! We gonna win! We're number one!"

Murray furrowed his brow and said, "What's with the 'we' stuff? You can't help on this one."

Before anyone could respond, I quickly jumped in. "Actually, Murray? Sean sort of can."

Everyone whirled around in my direction. I settled into an upholstered wing chair and delicately explained part two of my plan. "Josh said it was actually harder to pass the test to get on than to win once you are on. He himself missed getting on by one contestant. If Mary Flanagan hadn't been at the tryouts, he would have made it. She beat him in the semifinals."

"So what's to prevent someone from beating Murray?" De fretted.

"Well, I'm no board-certified physician, but I think a little preventive medicine should do the trick," I stated—a statement that was met with four pairs of upshot eyebrows.

"Excuse me, Cher. How could you possibly know that no one smarter is going up against Murray?" Amber asked.

"While I can't control the entire situation, I can take the advice in that famous poem Daddy always quotes, 'Like in baseball, Cher, you play the percentages.'"

De was all "You don't play baseball, Cher."

"True, girlfriend, but I am an excellent math student, and I calculate that if the overwhelming percentage of other *Jeopardy!* wannabes aren't up to Murray's level of trivia retention, wouldn't his chances of winning be solidly increased?"

"You're losin' me, Cher. How do we know who else is going up against Murray?" De said.

"Well, girls and boys," I explained calmly, "we can't know everyone, but we *can* know the first group he'll be tested with. Josh says that the test is done in stages. After a written test—which even Josh passed—they pick the best player from a group of three. What if Murray's backup team was say, I don't know, maybe Sean and Amber?"

Sean, no surprise, was clueless and didn't react. Amber, for once, was speechless. Her jaw totally dropped. It fell to De to give me my props. She got down on her knees and did a we're-not-worthy salute to my brilliance. Intrinsically, De understood what would happen in such a *Jeopardy!* tryout round. And who knew what step Sean would be up to in his Rodman Kit antics? No doubt, that would be enough to boot him from the finals—while Amber's haughty attitude would cancel her out. The contestant coordinators would be left with Murray: quick-witted, charm-enhanced, and smart. A total Kenneth Cole shoe-in!

Finally, Amber piped up. "What gives you the hubris to think we would agree to this?"

"Because it's for Murray, that's why, Amber. It's taking a stand for friendship and loyalty and showing how simpatico you really are under that . . . that patina of vinyl." Quickly I turned to De. "No, not the restaurant. It's a new word I learned."

Amber sighed. "Whatever, Cher. Say I do go along with this credibility-impaired scheme of yours. What exactly makes you think I won't win? I mean, excuse me, I'm not exactly brain-drained. If you think I would give a faux answer on purpose, you've got the wrong ringer."

I bit my tongue. Amber had so left herself open to a barrage of put-downs. But much as it pained me, I needed her. Murray needed her. So I simply shrugged my shoulders and said, "We'll take our chances, Amber. And may the best contestant win."

I instructed Murray to go straight home and present the plan to his father. On Monday I'd call the *Jeopardy!* office to get details about the teen tournament tryouts. Monday. My final cell phone day. I felt a pang of emptiness.

"De." I tapped her elbow as she and Murray headed for the door. The others had already left, and I needed a private interface with my main big. "A moment."

De disentangled herself from Murray. "Go on, sugar, I'll be right out." Then she turned to me. "Zup, Cher? Is there more to the plan you didn't want to say in front of the others?"

"Not exactly, De. I didn't say anything before because I wanted to keep Murray's meeting on point. But I did get some furiously dope news myself, and I totally have to share it with you."

I described my major coup at snaring the *Savvy* internship. De was beyond thrilled for me. "I'm kvelling! This calls for a celebration!" she whooped. "Cheesecake Factory at five o'clock! Treat's on me, girlfriend!"

The Cheesecake Factory is one of the trendiest eateries around. Located mainly in upscale suburbs, it features spiral-bound twelve-page menus with full-page advertisements for upscale clothiers. An admirably cutting-edge service to patrons who might want to peruse fashion while deciding on an entrée. Naturally, the Cheesecake Factory is most famous for its bodacious desserts—and the normal two-hour wait to get in. But they give you a beeper when you get there, so the waiting time can be productively spent trolling the mall. A stellar concept.

"Meet you there then." I gave De a hug as she left. Then I realized that this weekend would be my last personal credit-card splurge for a month. The emptiness pangs were coming closer together.

The big hand on my Gucci watch was on the twelve and the little hand on the seven when De and I were led to our table at the Cheesecake Factory. By then I'd had the most awesomely productive three hours, snaring several excellent ensembles. "How chronic is this stuff?" I asked rhetorically. "I just have to pick one for my debut at *Savvy* on Tuesday. First impressions are so crucial." I held up a microscopic Vivienne Westwood power suit. "The survey says . . . ?"

"You rule at *Savvy!* You'll be the most golden fashionista intern they have ever hired. Oh, wait, hang on, Cher. I brought one." De bent over to retrieve her Prada backpack, which she'd placed judiciously underneath the table. When she resurfaced, she held an advance copy of the new *Savvy*. "Hot off the presses," she said triumphantly, handing it to me.

"Girlfriend! Major snaps!" I said admiringly. "How'd you get your hands on this? I'm sure it hasn't hit the street yet."

"You have to ask? As you would say, Cher, it's like that famous poem, 'it totally pays to be well-connected.'"

Then I took a better look at the cover. The smoldering eyes of Antonio Sabato Jr. were staring seductively back at me. Antonio just so happens to be a client of De's mother, the most powerful public relations diva in an entire three-block area of Beverly Hills.

"You are so money, De!" I squealed. "Come, let us scan!"

We dissected *Savvy* as we dove into our spiced Thai chicken salads and angel hair primavera. We totally dished about every page. We just couldn't help ourselves, we came up with dozens of prime ideas to make *Savvy* even better than it already was.

Like, we'd never noticed it before? But there was no section devoted exclusively to designers. And it never bothered me previously, but where in the accessory section were the cutting-edge belt buckles, the Austrian crystals, to say nothing of the Chanel gold hair clips. And while the "In Shape" section did have worthy articles like the one I'd read on the Zone, I couldn't recall the magazine ever doing a piece on the aerobic benefits of mall trolling. Ideas were bouncing around our heads like microwave popcorn when it's been in too long. We were psyched!

"Let's make a list," I proposed, whipping out my electronic Franklin agenda hand-held notebook. "The top ten ways *Savvy* can be improved."

"Excellent! Cher, you walk in there with that on Tuesday, they're gonna elect you Editrix-in-Chief! Or Accessories Editor! Or Accessory to the Accessories Editor!"

"Tscha, De," I said modestly. "It's not about power. I just want to contribute. I never considered that having a job could be so fulfilling and such a rampant help to my impressionable *Savvy*-reading peers. And to think it was a bet with the step-drone that led me to this point. The world truly does work in mysterious ways."

I turned to a quiz-bearing page titled "Does He Secretly Worship You?"

"Look at these questions. 'Does he make excuses to cross your path more than three times a day?' Lame! A better one would be, 'Does he beep you incessantly?' "

All at once, a dread gloom washed over De. She was thinking about Murray. Instinctively, I reached out and took her hand. "It's going to be okay, De. Our plan for keeping Murray with us will work. You'll see."

But De was in distress. "What if the plan backfires? I mean, what if Amber's right and she cancels Murray out in the first round?"

"That's what you're buggin' about? Like Amber might win! As if! De, get a grip. Josh said it isn't only brain power that gets you on. Telegenics is fully key. In the battle for Are-you-someone-America-wants-to-see? you really think Amber's haughty is any match for Murray's pure sweetness and his brilliance?"

"My man is sweet," De agreed, but then she fretted. "That can only get him past the first round. We can't know who else he'll be up against in the finals."

"I'll allow that, De, but preparation is our first line of defense. Along with our spin-control ringers, we will commit to fully prepping Murray."

"How are we gonna do that, Cher?"

"What you just said: connections. We'll use our connections to bring in experts from all pertinent fields. The second Murray's father says it's a go, I'm enlisting our class president Brian Fuller as computer consultant for any tech questions Murray might have to answer, even if I have to cede my parking spot temporarily. Then I'll get Daddy to give Murray a quick course on law. You can drill him in everything showbiz, Mr. Hall and Miss Geist will contribute their expertise in their fields, and so on."

"You think all those people will help?"

"It's for *Murray*. Who's more beloved on the campus of Bronson Alcott? Present company excluded. So we get all our duck à l'orange in a row. And then, we take a leap of faith."

"A leap of faith?"

"Do you believe in Murray, De? He isn't my boyfriend, but I do, and I believe he will ace this and be back in his father's good graces and in the hallowed hallways of Bronson Alcott taking his rightful place among us."

De learned across the table, and we high-fived as she intoned, *"Hal'vai . . ."*

De's Yiddish plea did not go unanswered. On Monday we got a matching pair of chronic signs from above. The *Jeopardy!* office informed me that the teen tournament tryouts were just starting up. Then, cosign! In the afternoon, we got the most golden news of all: Murray's father approved our plan.

"It took me a solid forty-eight to wear him down," Murray explained, "but he finally agreed." Murray lowered his voice to imitate his father: " 'Your mother and I will allow you to show us what you have learned at that school, but you had better produce on this game show. And there are other conditions, son.' "

"What conditions?" De asked nervously.

"I gotta stem the tide of my grade point meltdown and take a Pasadena on school night events. If I screw up on any of the above, I'm gone, baby."

Murray's dad was being heinously Amish. I could see an errant tear forming in De's eye, so I jumped in with our solution-oriented tutorial plan.

All our teachers were rampantly supportive. Mr. Hall and Miss Geist prepared study guides in Shakespeare, American history, and protests of the '60s. I enlisted my enviro-warrior friend Mackenzie to teach Murray about the three R's—rain forests, recycling, and reduction. Brian Fuller was in charge of tech training, and my creative friend Summer was on the art patrol. Daddy agreed to bring in Chris Darden for that tricky it's-the-law category. De's mom said she could contact Beverly Sills just in case the rampantly horrifying opera category came up. I had a flash of panic when Murray said, "Why not just get Oprah herself? Why do we need some poser?"

In all the getting Murray ready-go-round, my own imminent debut nearly got obscured. It's like when you've only just flipped the calendar to December and hello, it's Hanukkah already. Tuesday arrived—*Savvy* day—and I wasn't close to prepared. I'd snagged all these chronic outfits, but *the* one hadn't presented itself fully to me. Ensembly indecisive, I lugged a selection of five, with accessories, to school. For the second time in less than a week, De sacrificed lunch to help. We used the teacher's lunchroom as a makeshift modeling area. First, I tried on a Todd Oldham.

"Dangerously overdressed," De decided. "It screams, 'I'm only doing this to win a bet. I don't really need to be here.'"

Then I modeled a Richard Tyler pin-striped suit. "Too businessy," she declared. "It's a teen magazine. I bet they're more casual."

"In what sense, De? Casual chic, casual retro, casual elegant, shimmer casual? Be specific."

"Simmer, Cher. Try this." De had chosen the Pixie

Yates knee-length sparkly brown denim skirt with the canary yellow crop-top cardigan and the criss-cross ankle-strap platforms.

That was a combo I hadn't considered, but as soon as I put it on, I could see De's eye for sartorial perfection had not been shrouded by her Murray woes. It was a total Shalom Harlow look, stellar for *Savvy*. "Righteous, De. Thanks."

Then De applied my makeup. To match my ensemble, she did me in burgundy and wine, highlighted with subtle, modern shimmer.

"Wish me luck, De."

"You don't need luck, Cher. You've got it all: your look, your list of ways to improve *Savvy*, and your natural enthusiasm. Not only are you going to contribute, in just thirty skinny days, you're going to meet three excellent college Baldwins. And just like you have faith in Murray, I have faith that one of them will be the hottie of your dreams."

As I would think about it later, and I often would, it would occur to me that, uncharacteristically, De was wrong. Or at least off by over twenty-nine days. For the day I walked into the offices of *Savvy* magazine was the day I met Matt.

Chapter 5

Matt wasn't the first person I saw when I arrived at the offices of *Savvy* magazine. That honor went to the receptionist. A pencil-thin Monet with that geek-chic look and winged specs, she ruled behind a huge Plexiglas panel. Its only opening was a narrow slot at the bottom for like shoving communiqués in and out. I wasn't sure if I could be heard through the bullet-proof glass, so I bent down and shouted into the slot, "I'm Cher Horowitz."

"And?"

I could see she was well practiced at faux indifference. I wondered if she'd treated Antonio Sabato the same way when he showed up for his interview. Clearly, she hadn't been prepped for my arrival, so I enlightened her. "I'm here for the internship program."

Wordlessly, she hit a buzzer underneath her desk and motioned for me to enter through the unmarked door to the right of her Plexiglas-encased kingdom.

Okay, so I'm not sure what I expected *Savvy's* office to look like. Only not this. Office decor was so not a strong suit. Instead of soft, muted lighting, huge private offices with picture windows overlooking L.A., it was furiously cubicle-riddled. Harsh light glared from fluorescent tubes beneath a dropped ceiling. Gauntlets of black and tan file cabinets obscured any wallpaper that might have added a sense of coziness.

"Wait here," the verbally minimalist receptionist instructed, pointing to a wooden chair in what functioned as a waiting area. "Someone'll be with you."

I used my waiting time productively. I whipped out my organizer with my How to Improve *Savvy* list, and made a subcategory for behind-the-scenes upgrades. I was just typing "distressed wood filing cabinets" when I heard his voice. Deep, distinctly male, he said, "You the new intern?"

I looked up and that's when I saw him. Involuntarily, I gasped. I was staring straight into the dark caramel eyes of the singularly most to-die-for studmuffin I have ever seen, on or off screen. Luckily, I caught myself in midswoon. I stammered, "Uh-huh." Because Amber wasn't there, I put myself down: Brilliant, Cher. First impressions are all that, and *that* was all lame.

A swatch of medium brown highlighted-with-gold lock of hair grazed his forehead. I resisted the urge to brush it back. His lips were full and lush, the kind women pay thousands to get. He turned and said, "Follow me." I wondered if everyone in this place was conversation-challenged. If so, in my present state I'd fit right in.

I tried to recoup my lost composure as I quickly shoved my organizer into my Coach backpack and did as instructed. The hottie was wearing stone-washed jeans, charmingly scuffed Timberland boots, and a tucked-in T-shirt, not ostentatiously tight but fitted enough to allow seriously well-defined cuts to peek through. I tried not to stare at his cute butt as I said, "I'm Cher. Do you, uh, have a job here?"

Without turning around, he said, "I'm an intern."

I quickly calculated: Daddy said all the interns were in high school. Check yes for age appropriate.

"So I guess that means we'll be interning together. What did you say your name was?" I tried for faux indifference but was pretty sure I didn't make it.

"Matt," he answered as he continued to lead me around a labyrinth of cubicles. Most were inhabited by fashion-impaired workers. I thought it was ironic that here I was at a teen fashion magazine and so far, not one designer ensemble had caught my eye. Come to think of it, we'd trolled like for miles, and not one supermodel or celebrity sighting either. I began to wonder if I hadn't accidentally wandered into the offices of *Rolling Stone* magazine.

Finally, Matt stopped walking. We'd reached our destination, the cubicle of one V. Nathanson, as the name plaque propped up on her desk advised.

"Here's the newbie you sent me to fetch," Matt said. "That it?"

"It is, my boy. You may return to the land of all things photographic." Grievously, he did, without further verbosity.

V turned out to be Vikki, and she turned out to be the boss of all interns. A way significant position for someone in what I calculated to be Gen-X age range— or on the precipice, anyway. Vikki had carrot-colored crispy hair, which she had paired with bright blue eye shadow; she was pushing the Mimi envelope. Sartorially, she was all the Dis-united Colors of Benetton, velvet jacket and skirt straight out of that K-whatever store. I heard her silent cry for a makeover.

"So, what's your name? Horowitz?" Vikki riffled through a stack of papers, one of several that spilled into each other and obscured her desk. She was chewing a prodigious wad of gum.

"Reporting for duty," I responded cheerily.

"I know the paperwork on you must be here somewhere. Take a load off, Horowitz."

I thought she meant help unload the clutter on her desk, but as I started to, she gave me a quizzical look and said, "No, I meant sit down." There was a chair squeezed into the corner of her cube office, and I cooperatively squeezed into it.

"Ever intern at a magazine before?" Vikki inquired.

"Not exactly. But I'm fully committed to reading them. In fact, I brought a list of ways *Savvy* could be improved."

"Did you?" Vikki asked, still shuffling papers and cracking her gum.

"I could read it to you," I offered.

Vikki looked up and laughed. "Not to dash your enthusiasm, Horowitz, but that won't be necessary. Let me explain how it works around here."

Then she described how each intern did a shift in each different department: Fashion & Beauty, In

Shape, Let's Get Quizzical, Art, Celebrities, Photography, and Goin' Postal. That last one had nothing to do with ballistic behavior but was the Letters to the Editor column.

"That way, you get to get coffee for all our editors," she quipped. "In fact, that's how I started. Now I edit Goin' Postal, and interns get coffee for me, see?" She brandished a bruised paper cup at me.

I smiled. "While I can see the benefits of that system, may I offer an alternative?"

Vikki stopped chewing and stared at me. That was my cue to continue. "Not to be immodest, but as you can probably see, fashion is my forte. The Fashion and Beauty section is where I could make the most bodacious contribution. I think that's where I should be placed for the duration of my internship."

Vikki reached into her mouth and withdrew her chewed-up gum. Spiriting it directly into a trash bin, she eyeballed me intensely and said, "Horowitz, you look like a bright girl, but I'm getting the impression you've never actually had a job before, am I right? Let me be the first to break it to you. Interns don't tell editors what they'd be good at or how *Savvy* can be improved—not the first day, okay? It might not be accepted in the most appreciative way, catch my meaning?"

I couldn't decide if Vikki had a latent urge to assert power or just a need to get to know me better. I reserved my opinion and decided to play along. "I'm fully catching it. By the way, what department is Matt in?"

She smiled knowingly. "Matt. Cute, huh?" Then she was all business. "Forget it, Horowitz. You're here to learn. I don't know how you even got in at this late date, and maybe you don't realize this, but hundreds of kids would give anything to be in your shoes."

"I know that," I said sincerely, glancing at my Steve Maddens and thinking of the entire populace of Bronson Alcott High School. "Being a role model is an awesome responsibility, and I take it very seriously."

Vikki didn't seem to comprehend. I was just about to explain, when out of nowhere a vigorous Gen-X Baldwin draped in excellent Armani threads appeared. Finally, someone with some style!

"Mr. G-Goldberg," Vikki stammered. "I didn't know you were in today. Did you need something?" I was surprised at her morph from gum-cracking casual to scarily subordinate.

"Just checking to see how this month's Goin' Postal column is coming along," he answered. "And it's Rick, remember?"

I glanced up. The look he gave Vikki said something way beyond editorial checkup. Although no one said so, I felt fairly certain slick Rick must be the nephew of Daddy's accountant. Which made him Vikki's boss. And even though I was, as Matt said, the newbie, I was also fairly certain sparks were flying between them. Or would have been if Vikki hadn't been too intimidated to catch fire.

When Rick walked away, Vikki abruptly got up and said, "Let's go, Horowitz. I'll find your paperwork later. You wanted to start in Fashion? It's yours. They're doing a shoot now. Follow me to the photo studio." Vikki led me through a set of double doors and down another corridor. When we got to the door marked

Photo Studio: Shoot in Progress, Vikki walked in without knocking. I was right behind.

The shoot in progress was two young models done in brown—the happening color—one in a Mark Wong Nark sleeveless chocolate-colored shift, the other in a cocoa V-neck wrap-top sweater and Armani Exchange hip huggers. They were posed up against a huge white backdrop. Instantly, my fashion sense kicked into high gear. While the ensembles were competent, if not cutting edge, the look lost it in accessories—way archival.

I was sure someone besides me could see the heinous mismatch. I scanned. The room was riddled with stylists, editors, a photographer-in-chief, and several assistants, plus two women I took to be the mothers of the models. Off in a corner, kneeling on the floor and loading film into a camera, was Matt. My heart totally skipped.

"Rossman! Hurry up and get that camera loaded!" the boss photographeress barked at Matt, who immediately launched up from his position and handed the fully loaded apparatus to her. He didn't see me.

With that break in the action, Vikki said, "I'm introducing you to Lila Sherwood. She's our top fashion editor. She'll be your boss for this rotation." Then she approached a severe editrix dressed for intimidation in a Richard Tyler power suit.

"Lila," she said cheerily, "got another intern for you. She's just starting today. Name's Horowitz."

Lila barely acknowledged me, so I extended my hand and said, "I'm Cher. In all like due respect? I think you should know that those accessories totally gag with that look." I went on to describe how if you're doing brown, earthy, edgy, and retro, the accessories need a complete overhaul. "I suggest geometric silver barrettes, not scrunchies, and instead of the backpacks, one girl should have a Cynthia Rowley mini tote."

Since Lila was regarding me with serious interest, I continued, "Readers should be able to look at those models and learn how to find their own style." I was totally quoting from the list De and I had made. I was sure Lila saw the positive aspects of my suggestions. That's why I was puzzled when she brutally brushed me aside, flipped her attention to Vikki, and flatly said, "I'm parched. Show her how to find the coffee machine. Tell her I take mine black."

As Lila trounced over to the models, Vikki suppressed a smile and motioned for me to follow her out of the photo studio. She walked me to the coffee machine, which was situated in its own cubicle. Then she said with a shrug, "Don't say I didn't warn you, Horowitz. Your best contribution will be coffee. Black, remember." With a wave, she turned on her heel and left.

I regarded the drip coffee maker. There were two decanters, one marked decaf and one regular. The misguided fashion editrix Lila hadn't specified. I was momentarily flummoxed, but then I thought about all the other people in the room, and of course about Matt. I bet he was parched, too. My instinct was to grab my cellular—but then I remembered the grievous ban. I looked around. Way serendipitously, there was a phone on the wall. I dialed nine—even in Daddy's home office, that's how you get an outside line—and called information for the closest Starbucks. Then I ordered up a lively selection of a dozen coffees: cappuccino, latte, double decafs, mochaccinos, espressos, and several in basic black. On the side, I opted for an assortment of biscotti, cinnamon sticks, and fat-free minimuffins. Starbucks said *Savvy* had a business account and did I want to charge the order? I may be a newbie, but I do know a legitimate business expense when I charge one. Besides, maybe once Lila came unparched, she'd be more receptive to my stellar suggestions for improving her fashion spread.

Not even. Okay, so I probably should have committed Vikki's intern-behavioral suggestions to memory. Grievously, my coffee-cum-nutrition largesse went furiously awry. When I re-entered the photo studio, Lila was rampantly engaged, bossing around the stylist, who gave heated instructions to the photographer, who totally barked at Matt. No one paid any attention to me until several minutes later, when Lila brushed by on her way to summon an assistant. Then she seemed to remember her coffee. Just at that moment the Starbucks delivery dude swung through the door balancing two boxes filled with my order.

Hello, you would have thought that Oasis brother spit on the stage at the Grammy Awards or something. It was massively volcanic the way Lila erupted at me. "What's the matter with you? Can't you even follow one simple direction? I told you to get me black coffee, not feed an army!" She turned to her assistant. "Get Nathanson in here. Get *her* out of my department!"

Everyone was staring at me. I was such the cheese. And then I heard a deeply masculine voice. Tentative, yet sincere. Nervous, yet committed. Hesitant, yet heroic. "She . . . was just trying to be nice. It's her first day. Maybe we could cut her some slack, okay?"

Suddenly everyone turned to stare at Matt. He'd totally crossed the picket line for me. I don't think Lila saw the valiant heroism in his act, because she whirled around on her five-inch Manolo Blahniks and shot dangerous daggers at Matt. "Oh, *this* is just what I need when I'm on deadline! The revolt of the interns! Look—whatever your name is. She shouldn't be trying to do anything except what I tell her to do! And you should keep your opinions to yourself!" Lila thundered. "This shoot is over." With that, she flounced out and slammed the door. Her flair for drama was exceptionally on point.

I drove home in a sweat. This must be what total mobile phone withdrawal feels like. I could not wait to tell De about my first day in the real world. I practically did that severe tire damage thing as I screeched into our driveway, rushed past Daddy, and dove for the phone next to my bed. "Dionne!" I was so relieved when she answered right away. "You will not believe what happened on my first day!"

De guessed it had something to do with my outfit, but not even. "I met him!"

"You met who?"

"Just like you said, the hottie of my dreams! He *was* out there—in the real world."

"Details!" De screamed into the phone.

"What can I say? A studmuffin of major proportions."

"In what sense? Sabato? Beck? Pitt?"

I considered. "I'd really have to go with Brad for the

cute, Beck for the lips, total DiCaprio in intensity, with a dollop of Cruise for heroics."

"Cruise-ly heroics? Were you drowning or merely being crushed by a horde of fans, Cher?"

Then I told De about my coffee contretemps. "I was just thinking globally, only Madame Fashionista wanted me to act locally. As in: just for her. But Matt so deeply understood and rushed to my defense."

De was with me. When I'd finished describing my day, she caught me up on the Murray train-your-brain express, which was right on track. After we hung up, I spent the rest of the night deciding what to wear for tomorrow's follow-up appearance at *Savvy*. Like that famous bumper sticker, I only braked for homework.

Chapter 6

I felt rampantly confident as I waved jauntily to the receptionist on my second day at *Savvy*. A confidence that, as it turned out, was woefully misplaced. Not only did the borderline-mute receptionist still not know who I was, but when I reported to Vikki's cubicle, she ruefully informed me that I'd been ejected from the Fashion & Beauty rotation. My attempt at generosity had viciously eclipsed any chance I had at contributing there.

On the up side, Vikki was beyond simpatico. "I take at least half the rap for yesterday's flame-out," she said sincerely, cracking her gum. "I should've warned ya Lila was on deadline."

"And that would be like an army of PMS invaders?" I guessed.

"Let's just say she's tightly wound. When I was an

intern she almost had me fired for *walking* too loudly on deadline day."

I would have recommended a tension-reduction aromatherapy soak, but I assumed that recommendations were probably still a no-no. So I went with, "I hope my bad didn't affect Matt."

Vikki hadn't been made aware of any negative repercussions Matt faced for his heroic intervention on my behalf. She checked her schedule. "No, he's still in photography." Then she glanced through some charts and mused, "Let's see. How about we try you in the art department today? They could use another hand down there. And, Horowitz—try to keep your suggestions to yourself. Although for the most part, our art directors are a fairly laid-back bunch."

"And my job would consist of getting coffee for them?" I guessed.

"Probably not. Most of them are Snapple drinkers." Vikki winked at me.

I had a feeling that my relationship with Vikki had undergone a momentous transformation, that somehow my bad had ingratiated me with her and she'd silently decided to mentor me here at *Savvy*. She did mention that she was once such the cheese. I suddenly felt an overwhelming urge to bring something to the relationship. So I did.

"Vikki, before we go to the art department, is it okay if I share a teensy observance with you?"

"What?" she asked suspiciously.

"I know as a newbie I'm supposed to be seen and not heard? But what I saw and heard yesterday is something you should be aware of. Trust me, this is something I've got real expertise in. You know that

Armani dude who said call him Rick yesterday? My relationship radar tells me he's got it bad for you."

"We confiscate radar detectors here, Horowitz," Vikki quipped, but then she got serious. "Look, I know you think you're being helpful, but this is another no-interns-allowed area."

"But I'm not speaking as an intern. This is a woman-to-woman thing. Rick is a Baldwin with serious style and wicked potential, and you totally didn't acknowledge him. Playing hard to get is one thing, but you weren't even suited up. Unless you're otherwise involved?"

Vikki sighed. "Let's put it this way. My Saturday nights *are* usually involved—with *Dr. Quinn, Medicine Woman*. But hold your horses, Horowitz." She dug into her bag for another piece of gum.

I wondered if hold your horses was like take a load off.

"A, this is none of your business—on any level—and B, this is completely nuts. Even if there was a shred of truth to this . . . observation of yours, it's not gonna happen. There's no way I could get involved with Mr. Goldberg. For one thing, he's my boss, which means he's out of my league. And if I tried anyway and it didn't work out, which office relationships never do, I'd get fired. Or quit. Neither of which is exactly a career option right now. And on the subject of inter-office relationships, add this to your list of new things to memorize. The same goes for intern-to-intern romances."

I was about to say how it was different with Matt and me. He was my total potential soul mate. So that inny-outy office stuff didn't pertain to us. But then Vikki added mysteriously, "Look, I know he's cute, Horowitz, but trust me on this. You don't want to get involved. Matt comes with some heavy baggage."

I was trying to picture what type of luggage Matt would carry, when I realized Vikki meant emotional baggage. That could only mean one thing: Matt needed me.

Vikki saw the look of serious concern on my face. "Just be sure to put my advice in the recycle bin on the way out," she deadpanned.

Savvy's art department, as Vikki advertised, was furiously casual. Forget offices, this department didn't even have cubicles. Located one level down from the editorial floor, it was one giant open-air bull pen riddled with artists and the tools of their trade: computers, printers, copiers, and other machines I didn't immediately recognize. Torn jeans and ragged pony tails were, like, the gold standard. Complaint music ruled. I guess it helped inspire the creative types down there, just like the operating room music on *ER*.

Vikki introduced me to Jim, the artist I'd be assisting. He was about twenty-five, with highly defined cheekbones and shoulder-length dark blond hair. He was massively engrossed in a computer game of Mah-Jongg.

"Slow news day?" I quipped as Vikki waved good luck and left.

Not taking his eyes off the computer screen, Jim said, "Yeah, I'm waiting for some slides to come down from photography before I can start on a layout. Meantime"—he looked up at me—"there's a laser layout coming out of printer six over there." He pointed it out. "Do me a favor. Grab it and make three copies, okay?"

An actual non-java-intense chore. "I'll get right on it!" I said a little too enthusiastically.

Jim looked at me strangely and went back to his game.

I retrieved the lasers and scouted out the photocopier. The nearest one was being used by a girl with long auburn hair, wearing a Bisou Bisou shift and black buckled boots. An admirably together look, from the back anyway. When she swung around, she regarded me curiously and said, "Are you the new intern? Cher Horowitz? The one who made Lila go ballistic yesterday?"

"Was that like our top story on today's interoffice memos?"

She laughed and extended her hand. She was wearing Hard Candy Virtual Violet nail polish. I could see a potential bond mate. "I'm Christie. This is my second tour as an intern here. Let me give you a tip. Office gossip travels faster than a Courtney Love image change. But don't stress, Cher. We're an equal opportunity gossip mill. We all get our turn at being today's news object. Just like we all get our turn at this."

Christie held up what she'd been copying. It was a printout of a layout as it would appear on a page of *Savvy*. It featured photos of six girls caught off guard in heinous fashion faux pas. I scanned for Amber.

"The Fashion Flops page?" I asked.

"And we all take turns posing for it, Cher."

"Not even." I studied her to see if she was like

kidding. She wasn't. "That one's me," she pointed out proudly.

I looked closely at the photo of the girl with her slip showing. "No way!"

"Way. Probably next month will be your turn."

Probably next month I won't be here is what I could have said but didn't. Instead I stammered, "Isn't that like harassment or something? I mean, forcing impressionable interns to pose in highly embarrassing ensembles?"

"Cher?" Christie said uncertainly. "I take it this is your first job. Welcome to the real world and lighten up."

Just then I heard my name being called from the other end of the room. "Yo, intern girl! Cher! Got those copies yet? My slides are here and I need them." It was Jim.

"Catch you later, Christie—and, uh, thanks for the tips."

I quickly made the copies and started to rush them over to Jim. I got to his desk just in time to see Matt turning around to leave. He stopped when he saw me. If it was possible, he looked even hotter than he had yesterday. He was wearing a deep blue denim button-down shirt and black jeans.

"Hi, Matt," I managed coyly, batting my eyelashes and handing Jim his photocopies. "I was hoping to bump into you today, since I didn't get a chance to thank you for the major props you did for me yesterday."

Matt shrugged his prodigious shoulders. "No biggie, Cher."

"Oh, but it was," I insisted. "You totally took a bullet for me."

Matt seemed unsure of a response, so I went with, "I guess you're Jim's slide deliverer?"

"I am. The first bunch of slides Jim had for the layout weren't happening, so they did a new photo shoot this morning. I'm delivering the new ones and taking back the old ones. Want to see?" he asked.

"Absolutely!" I had no clue what it was I just said I wanted to see.

"Come by the light box," he instructed, leading me to a table with a built-in fluorescent. Matt gingerly placed six slides down on it, side by side.

"Hang on. I'll get a viewer," he said, lifting a mini-binocular-like thing from the nearest unoccupied artist's desk. Matt positioned the viewer over a slide and leaned over the light box to look at it. "Here, you look now," he said, moving over slightly to make room for me.

I leaned over. Then Matt inched closer to me. It was a furious mind over Matt-er moment. My mind was all, Concentrate on what he's saying! but my body was all, Ultimate thrill! I totally inhaled him. His aura was majorly all boy.

"These are the rejects," Matt was explaining.

The slides were of yesterday's models from the photo session I'd inadvertently disrupted. "Did I do something to cause their grievous rejection?"

"No, you had nothing to do with it," he said. "The reason these are rejects is because the lighting was off. Look closely, Cher, and you'll see there are shadows across this model's face."

Matt was right. The model's face looked like Cruella de Vil's hair, a lighting catastrophe where one side came out way darker than the other. I went to pick up another slide.

"Careful, Cher," Matt warned gently. "It's very easy to smudge a slide with your finger by accident, so you always put it in a slide sheet—like this." He picked up an eight-by-ten transparent holder, which resembled something you'd cover a report with, only it had these twenty cute little windowettes where slides could be slotted in.

Matt went on to explain other aspects photographic. He was all animated as he dropped tidbits about cropping and composition.

"I'm seriously impressed, Matt. You learned a lot as an intern."

"Yeah, right," he said caustically. "I've learned pretty much zilch here. I knew this stuff going in. Photography's kind of my thing. I've been into it ever since I was a kid."

"Are you taking pictures for *Savvy?*"

"I'm an intern, remember? The most they let me do is load the camera, fetch props, and be a messenger between the photo studio and the art department."

"So they're not actually teaching you anything about photography?"

"Want to know what I've learned here?" Matt's smile revealed deep-dish dimples. It was way heart-melting. "All they ever say to me is, 'Rossman, be careful with that film!' Like the worst thing anyone could ever do is lose track of a slide, especially if it's earmarked for a layout. That's why, even when they're in the slide sheets, you've gotta hold them from the top. The slides in the top row have been known to fall out. And they never send them down to the art department through those interoffice mail envelopes. All slides are hand delivered. That way they know who to fire if something's lost."

"So like losing a slide is worse than overordering cappuccino?" I quipped flirtatiously.

"Grounds for immediate dismissal and maybe for being sued." Matt went back to his serious posture.

"Don't worry," I said gravely. "My father's a totally prominent attorney."

Matt didn't answer. Did he think I was bragging? Maybe here in the real world, the rules are skewed. I quickly brought the conversation back to him.

"So how come you're so photogenically—I mean, photographically—enhanced? Do you come from a long line of famous photographers or something?"

Matt laughed. That smile again. "Hardly. But I hope to be one eventually."

"Like Herb Ritts?" I guessed, but I could tell by the look on Matt's face that photographing fashion models probably wasn't his dream. I repaired the damage with the way complimentary "I bet you take bodacious pictures. Did you have to present, like, a portfolio of your best stuff to get this job?" Daddy did say that only highly qualified kids were eligible for internship positions.

Matt checked his watch. Always a less than positive sign. "Uh, I'd better go," he said, collecting the slides. "They're probably about to send a search party. Later, Cher."

* * *

Later actually came sooner. Same day, in fact, outside *Savvy*'s offices at the elevator. I'd just pressed the down arrow button when Matt emerged from the office. He was wearing a significantly lived-in leather jacket and carrying a battered and bruised generic backpack. I noticed the latest issue of *Savvy* peeking out of the top.

"Studying up for tomorrow?" I asked, pointing to the magazine.

"Uh, no. This is for my sister," he said shyly.

"Younger?" I guessed.

He only nodded, but something struck me about his nod. "How old is she?"

Call me mental, but I know what I saw: deep pools of sadness in his caramel eyes as he mumbled, "Uh, she'll be eleven." Matt looked the way Daddy sometimes does when he talks about Mom.

"What's her name?" I asked.

"Monica."

"Do you have a picture—one you took?"

Matt furrowed his brow. "Not on me."

Under normal circumstances, this was grievously early in the relationship, but I broke my own rules to offer, "The Caffeine Café is a few blocks from here. Want to try again at that cappuccino?"

"Thanks, but I really gotta get home" was all he said. Okay, so maybe I was playing it too enthusiastically.

As I pulled out of the parking lot and drove up to the light, I caught a glimpse of Matt, walking down the block . . . toward the bus stop?

On the cellularless drive home, I evaluated. Today had been a day of furious progress. I was getting closer to Matt, and I didn't make anyone go ballistic. Memo to Josh: I am so successing at this real world job stuff! Memo to Rico, our family chauffeur slash pool engineer: Please gas up my Jeep, as I am temporarily credit card challenged—and put the tab on Daddy's bill. Memo to self: Find out if Matt's car is in the shop.

Chapter 7

*I*t's faux! Like the flying cow scene in *Twister*," I said. De, Amber, and I had gotten out of chemistry, since there was a substitute teacher who bought our story about an emergency student council caucus. We were sunning ourselves at the south end of the Quad. I wasn't being a traitor by revealing *Savvy*'s deep, dark secret about the Fashion Flops page. Hello, if you can't tell your t.b.'s, who can you tell? So I explained how it's not a stealth operation where they ambush fashion victims on the street and photograph them as everyone has always thought.

"How faux?" Amber, who'd obviously harbored a way justified fear of opening up the new issue of *Savvy* and finding herself among the Fashion Flops, anxiously asked.

"Like any of Tori Spelling's body parts, okay? Feel better now?"

To Amber's major "Whew!" I added, "Here's another tidbit that will make your day, Amber: they use interns for the feature. They dress them—that is, us—up in garish attire and then pose us with even more heinous accessories."

Amber licked her chops. "Which means next month's issue is a keeper!"

I would have figured out a way to personally avoid that bit of humiliation, but I had more pressing matters to deal with. Specifically: Matt. It was like that classic twelve-step nursery rhyme—one giant step forward, two baby steps back. In spite of the prodigious progress I'd made since we met, it had been, like, a *week* and we hadn't budged. We were still on majorly superficial interoffice terms. Because Amber was with us, I almost didn't say anything, but after about five minutes, I could hold back no longer. I bolted up from my reclining position.

"De, I am so frustrated! This must be what it feels like to call every branch of Neiman's and not one has your size in the exact color you need." Not that I could order anything over the phone anyway, I realized with a pang. Being plastic-deprived is *so* un!

"I feel your pain," De said sympathetically as she turned her face directly toward the sun. "Exhale, girlfriend."

I let it all out. "It's like, I am so close with Matt. I can so feel how right we are for each other. And I know he feels it too. Like why else would he defend my coffee-getting honor? And why else would he give me that in-depth course on slide composition? I mean, as if boys do that for every random Betty. He's close to smitten, I can feel it. So why are we not moving closer?"

"Okay, Cher. Dr. Dionne is in," she said, sitting up to acknowledge the gravity of my situation. "Let's analyze. Describe your relationship."

I took a deep breath. "Whenever I accidentally on purpose bump into him, we totally interface. He's always interested, sincere, sweet. Flirty even. And way animated, but usually when he's talking about F-stops, backdrops, and stuff. It's like the safety topic. I try to steer us into more personal waters, but he won't go there. He clams. It's like what Nala says about Simba in *The Lion King:* 'He's holding back, he's hiding—but what? I can't decide.'"

De was all "I remember that scene. Cher, that is way tragic."

"Especially since Matt is my ideal boyfriend. Potentially."

Amber, sensing an opportunity to diss me, sprung to life. "Excuse me, your ideal boyfriend? How could you know that? You just said you don't know anything about him."

"I know the need-to-knows," I said reflexively.

"Really, Cher?" Amber injected. "Pop quiz: what kind of car does he drive?"

Matt headed toward the bus stop last week. I cringed.

"Don't know, do you? What is more elemental in a relationship?" Amber demanded. Unsurprisingly, she wasn't finished. "Where does he live?"

I cringed again. Amber rapid-fired away, "What

school does he go to? What's his credit card max? Hilfiger or Hugo Boss? Hush Puppies or JP Tods? Joe Boxers or Calvin briefs?"

Even De was stunned by my silence. She whispered, "Cher, do you even know what kind of music he likes?"

Defensively, I crossed my arms in front of my chest. "Okay, I'll allow that I might be somewhat detail-deficient. But I do know this: Matt is special. He's not *like* any other Baldwin I have ever known. This could be it, the real deal."

Just at that moment, Murray and Sean, who should have been in study period, came loping over the horizon. Murray lit up when he saw De and was inspired to crack witty. "Looky who's here, the three divas—Luciano AMBER-otti, Placido DE-mingo, and Jose CHER-reras!"

"Murray rocks opera!" I squealed admiringly.

"No, no, Cher. That would be *Evita* or *Tommy*," he knowledgeably rejoined.

"Tommy who?" Sean asked, perplexed.

"The Who's *Tommy*," Murray corrected.

Sean gave up trying to figure that out and was all "What's goin' on?" as he totally plopped down next to Amber. "You ladies cut class to plot how Cher's gonna rule *Savvy?*"

"Correction," De said. "We never cut class. We were excused. It's in our contracts that whenever there's an understudy, we don't have to make an appearance in that particular class. We're plotting how Cher's gonna get next to Matt. She thinks he might be . . . the one."

Murray raised his hand. "Excuse me for casting

aspersions on your romantic field of dreams, Miss Cher, but have I not heard that before?" Then Murray went all Alex Trebekian. "Contestants, the category is He's the One, by Cher Horowitz. For one hundred dollars, the clue is: Buff workout trainer who was only using her."

Amber did a faux buzzer click. "Who is . . . Buff Bobby!"

Murray was all, "Give the lady her money! Now, for two hundred dollars: Romeo who Cher-as-Juliet ended up having nothing in common with."

Sean was getting the hang of it now. "Who is Skyler Handler!"

"My man!" Murray high-fived Sean. "Okay, so now for three hundred dollars: He had her, babe, until he found out she was only in high school."

De, who misplaced her supportive streak, was all "Who is Sonny!"

"That's my woman! She knows her men! Now we've got an Audio Daily Double! For five hundred dollars, listen carefully to the clue." I could not believe it. Murray did a dead-on imitation of Aldo, the Italian exchange student I'd fallen for, okay, not that long ago.

While a part of me had to give Murray snaps for his focus on the game, like hello? A Rolodex of my archival boyfriends? I had to stop this before we got into the Double Jeopardy round and Murray remembered Kip Kilmore, Scott Morrison, or worse, dug up my third-grade crush, Chip Mandelbaum.

"Okay! Hello, you've made your point. Like you've pummeled your point. Maybe I have had some false alarms in the past, but I am so over all of them. I was immature then. Now that I'm in the real world, I'm head over feet for Matt. And if you were real friends, you'd help me figure out what to do." Even to my own ears, I sounded pouty. Which is so not me.

De was all, "Cher's serious, guys. She's a smitten kitten."

Murray was all, "Meow! So like, hello kitty. What's the problem? You're usually catnip to your victims, Cher. Scratchin' up the wrong post this time? Metaphorically speaking, of course."

Then De detailed my situation, weighing in with, "Maybe Matt really does have it bad for you, only he's afraid to commit. It's a classic male-hood disease."

"I got it!" Sean said. "Maybe he can't reveal himself to you because he's in the witness protection program! I saw it on *NYPD Blue*, there was this dude—"

Murray needed no encouragement to jump right onto Sean's chain-of-fools thought process. "Oh, no, wait, he's an amnesiac! That's it! He don't know who he is—that's why he can't tell Cher!"

Murray and Sean were on a roll. They traded ridiculosities. "He's a twin! Yeah, that's the ticket! I saw it on *Sister, Sister!* He's inconsistent because he's two different people and one don't know what the other said!"

"No, no, wait! I got it, bro! He's an alien! Like one of them *Men in Black* aliens, living among us, all peaceful like. Cher! See if he can rip his head off! Then you'll know."

Somewhere in the distance, a bell rang. I checked my Piaget. It was time for next period, Hall's class.

Unsurprisingly, Amber had to buzz in with the last

82

word. As she got up and dusted herself off, her parting shot was "The top three reasons you can't get anywhere with Matt? One: he's already involved with someone else."

I shuddered. Amber continued, "Two: he just doesn't like you. Or three—and this is my personal favorite—he's out of your league. Cher, he's just too hottie to handle."

As if! "They haven't made the hottie who's too—" I started, but De cut me off. "Why waste energy on the nonessential Amber Salk? Let's bolt. We'll continue in Hall's class."

Next period, De and I fully ruminated over the possible reasons I was failing in my bid to snare Matt. We only stopped long enough to catch Amber's presentation of "Still waters run deep," the quote Mr. Hall had assigned us to define.

Amber had managed a quick change of outfits between our refresher pause and class. She was now all tropical Barbie, in rain forest halter top and some amphibian-themed micro-mini skirt. Standing next to Hall's desk, she began dramatically. "Still waters run deep, by Amber Salk. When I was in the Caymans, I went snorkeling? And Daddy specifically said, 'Princess, it's too deep out there. Don't go past the coral reefs.' But I didn't pay attention. I looked so yummy that all the little fishes in the sea were enamored. They stared at me with those big fish eyes. And then, before I knew it? I tried to touch the bottom and I couldn't feel it! I'd accidentally wandered out into deep waters! The moral of the story? Daddy always knows best!"

I don't think I've ever seen Mr. Hall's fish eyes go any

bigger than they did just then. He was too stunned to respond to Amber's trivial interpretation. Which she took as an A, and jauntily flounced back to her seat.

All Hall could manage was, "Sean? I believe you're next."

Sean ambled up to the front of the room, gripping a handful of charts, maps, and spreadsheets. Way Ross Perot, except without the ears. He began. "Mr. Hall? In all like, due respect, I think they made a mistake. They all meant, 'Still waters *are* deep.' And I did some research on that. This one's for my man, Murray. Listen up, they might ask you this on *Jeopardy!* At its deepest point, the Atlantic Ocean is 28,000 feet, or 8,530 meters. Now, you compare that to the Pacific—that's the one by us. It goes 36,198 feet deep, or 11,033 meters. We got them beat by—"

"Sean!" Mr. Hall interrupted and began massaging his temples. "That will be enough. Does anyone have an aspirin?"

Thirty pairs of hands flew into designer backpacks with offerings of various prescriptives for what ailed Mr. Hall. I turned to De and sighed. "Is there a pill for what ails my relationship with Matt?"

Which Amber overheard. "Why don't you just do what you always do, Cher? Send yourself flowers or Godiva. Pretend—and I accent the word *pretend*—someone else actually likes you. Maybe then you'll get picture-boy's attention."

De was all "Okay, Cher, we've studied this from every angle. Here's my suggestion. Go with the photo thing. If that's what flutters his shutter, go with it, girlfriend. If he opens up about that, maybe he'll open up about other things."

I was kind of surprised De would resort to advice like that. "Way Jurassic, De. Like that lame advice they used to give girls; pretend to be interested in what he's interested in."

De shrugged. "What can I say Cher? I'm not telling you to join Photo Shop. Just get the boy to open up, that's all. Hey, girlfriend, it's a plan."

Then De thought of something else. "If all else fails, go to plan B: get him to do one of those revealing *Savvy* quizzes with you."

Over the next few days, I was all Project Matt. I was determined to get to know him better—and vice mega versa. He'd rotated out of photography and was now the intern at In Shape. Vikki had spun me off into her domicile, Goin' Postal, where I continued to observe Rick stopping by her desk with one pathetic excuse after another.

I was profoundly excellent at making up excuses of my own—the sole purpose of which was to finagle my way into In Shape. Every time I opened a letter from a reader—or wrote my own—needing aerobic advice, I hand delivered it to Matt's department. The In Shape editor, Stacee Davis, was much more accommodating than Fashion & Beauty's drama queen. Stacee actually sat down with the letters and hand wrote her answers. Which gave me several windows of opportunity to interface with Matt. I flung open as many as I could.

"So, are you, like, getting school credit for this internship?" I asked, hoping to find out what school he went to. Matt seemed confused, so I offered, "At Bronson Alcott, where I go, they sometimes give you credit for worthy electives like this."

"Is that why you're here?" Matt turned his gentle gaze on me.

"Oh, no. I'm here . . ." I didn't want to tell him about my bet with Josh, so I went, " . . . for the real world—that is, actual job—experience."

Matt shrugged. "Well, I'm here for the actual financial experience."

Was there a finance department for budding CFOs? Then it hit me like a stack of Manolo Blahnik boots falling off the shelf in my closet. I heard Josh's taunting, "Some people your age have jobs because they need the money!" Matt was a total one of those. And it made me love him even more.

But hello? Matt had to need more than he was getting here. I mean, if all interns are created equal and stuff, he was getting what I was getting. Which was mainly, when I opened my first paycheck, a surprise. It was way number-enhanced, only like that famous poem, it signified pretty much nothing. Some dude with the initials FICA got most of it.

Day by day, more compatibility stuff leaked out. He was seventeen. We both liked a musical cornucopia of alternative, hip-hop, and mainstream. And, sign! We were both closet *Lion King* fans. But it seemed like every time we hit on something as deep as that, Matt would pull away. He'd suddenly remember something he had to do or somewhere he had to be. Sort of like before Lois knew Clark was Superman.

Try as I might, I could not get his digits; grievously, he never asked for mine. Nor did he make any attempt to explore an out-of-office relationship. Every time I proposed something like getting together on the weekend, he found a reason to say no. Like one night, I made sure to leave at the same time Matt did. As the elevator doors closed in front of us, I ventured, "I noticed that maybe, uh, your car's in the shop or something?"

"What?" Matt was momentarily confused and brushed back that rebellious runaway lock of hair that kept falling in his face. I couldn't tell if he knew I'd been scoping his bus stop habits. "I take the bus," he finally answered.

"Well, if you're not committed to public transportation, I could give you a lift." I tried to keep it majorly casual.

"That's not a good idea, Cher," Matt said as we got to the ground floor.

"Why not?"

"Hey, look, it's really nice of you and all, but . . . I gotta go." With that, the hottie of my dreams bounded away from me as fast as he could. I checked my compact. Was there an unsightly stain on my collar? Was Matt secretly calling me Cher Horo-shmutz?

I didn't have as much time as I would have liked to obsess about that. The *Jeopardy!* tryouts were upon us, and we had to get Murray prepped. There were last-minute tutorials, as well as the all-important what-to-wear crises to deal with.

Because of prior commitments on my time—that is, my after-school job at *Savvy*—I couldn't physically be there with Murray, De, Amber, and Sean. But I was fully spiritually available. Since I was still in the cellular-free zone, I could only call De for updates when I was near a phone. This was so *Little House on the Prairie!* Still, I made it my business to be near stationary phones often.

The first time I made De contact, she told me that Murray had taken my wardrobe advice and gone Diesel, while Sean had taken his own advice and gone with the oversize purple velvet brimmed cap and matching velvet bell-bottom pants. And then there was Accessorize-Me Amber: she was sporting a creamy leather patch over her left eye. While trying on a pair of sunglasses at the Donna Karan sample sale, an inventory tag brutally stuck her in the eye. There was no permanent damage except the lawsuit Amber's father was inflicting on the tag company.

De's second update was way positive. Murray, Sean, and Amber had all aced the written part of the test, in which Alex himself, live on video, asked the questions. Our buds were among the chosen few asked to stay for part two: the mock game. So far? Everything was going exactly as I'd planned it.

De's third bulletin was even more encouraging. As predicted, Amber walked out on the mock game, pronouncing it brutally faux. "Excuse me, Alex was AWOL. There were pathetic underlings reading the questions. It was a mockery," she'd huffed. Then De described Sean as he resurfaced next. "Our second ringer looked like he'd been through the ringer."

The fourth and final time I got to call her, Murray himself answered the cellular. "Nailed it, Cher! I had no problem with the categories. I just gotta work on my buzzer rhythm, that's all."

* * *

And as it turned out? Murray had no problem with his assessment. A few days later, De called with a golden this-just-in. "Cher, put on your backless Calvin! Murray and I are taking you out to dinner!"

"Which could only mean—"

"Girlfriend, it worked! Sean and Amber didn't get the call, but my man did. Murray is officially part of *Jeopardy!*'s teen tournament, and tonight we are celebrating big time!"

Chapter 8

*I*f all else fails, Cher . . ." I was obsessing over Matt, when De's prophetic words came back to me. Tragically, all else *had* failed. I did passive-aggressive and sent myself flowers to make Matt think some other Baldwin was crushing on me. I did aggressive-passive, suggesting a Saturday afternoon of Rollerblading for two where I could wipe out adorably and Matt could rescue me. But it was all nix on the chick tricks. Matt was foliage-oblivious and begged off the skate-date, sighing, "Wish I could, Cher, but I've got plans."

Reluctantly, I checked with my internship-bud Christie to find out if another Betty had dibs on Matt, but she wasn't aware of any liens on his affections. Amber's jagged little "maybe he just doesn't like you" theory came up on me like Johnny Rockets' French fries, but every time I considered that maybe Ambulame had a point—besides her pointy last semester Nine Wests—Matt would do something *so* vigorously sweet. Like the other day? He brushed my bangs back when we were huddling by the copy machine. And later? When we passed each other at the interoffice mail bin, he was all "Wow, you look great, Cher." I was wearing my midnight blue velvet overalls. And then? At the elevator? The way he looked at me? Hello, Matt was dropping hints like Ambu-losis drops breath mints.

And yet we were still not aboard the couplehood express.

I had no choice but to go to Plan B—De's "make him take a *Savvy* quiz" idea. To make that happen in the least obvious manner, I had to tap into my relationship with my mentoress, Vikki. She alone had the power to rotate Matt and me into a week-long gig of togetherness, interning side by side in *Savvy's* Let's Get Quizzical department, a way natural environment for me to quiz him.

Over the last few days, Vikki and I totally bonded. She was teaching me the basics of the Goin' Postal column, and I was opening her eyes to the concept that she and Rick could work—and to eye makeup that was a little less invasive. Even though I was woefully credit-card challenged, we'd even made a wardrobe slash makeup upgrade shopping date for later in the week.

While it pained me to milk our relationship for personal gain, I saw no other possibility. So I checked my pride at the cubicle and totally begged her.

"So, what do you think, Vikki? Can my next rotation be in Let's Get Quizzical? And can, like, Matt's be, too?

Sometimes you use two interns at the same time in a department."

Vikki was all "Don't you ever give up, Horowitz?"

"Give up on Matt? How can I? He's the yin to my yang. Potentially."

Reluctantly, Vikki agreed to check her intern-rotation charts. "Okay, let's see if it's even remotely viable. Rossman . . . Rossman . . . which departments hasn't he worked in yet?"

As she mused, I mentally scribbled, "Cher and Matt Horowitz-Rossman cordially invite you to . . ."

"Well, Horowitz," Vikki finally said, glancing up at me, "you might be in luck. Rossman hasn't worked in Quizzes yet, so it seems doable."

Doable. I could not have put it better myself. I jumped up. "Vikki, I will so never forget this. You have a stylist for life—not to mention a t.b.," I said sincerely, and gave her a hug.

The editor of Let's Get Quizzical had scored a windowed cubicle, which meant she was impressively high up on the *Savvy* food chain. As it turned out, however, she was nowhere in sight when I reported for my first day. But, yes! Matt was. He'd already made himself comfortable, leaning back in a chair, his Timberlanded feet propped up on a desk next to where he'd parked his ever-present camera. Matt appeared to be thumbing through a prodigious stack of *Savvys*, so I couldn't tell if he was impressed by my fetching new BeBe minidress and stylish high-top boots. He did smile when he looked up, though.

"Are you in quizzes this week, too?" I said, feigning

surprise. Those acting classes I took last semester totally paid off.

"I am," he said, swinging his feet off the desk. "I was wondering if we'd ever be in the same department. At the same time, that is."

"I guess our time is now," I said, doing nonchalance 101. "Is there an editor we're supposed to get coffee for or something?"

Matt grinned. "Yolanda Garcia is in charge of this department, and no, she didn't say anything about coffee. She had to bolt for a meeting, so she just told me to go through a bunch of old issues and come up with ideas for a male point of view for a new quiz."

Stellar! This was playing out better than even I could have planned it. There was a desk directly across from the one Matt was at. I claimed it and said with a wink, "I've got a better idea."

"Good, because to be honest, from what I've read so far, I think these quizzes are dumb. I was hoping to avoid this department and maybe do a double rotation in Photography. I thought I had it set, but when I came in today, Vikki said I had to be here. It was unavoidable."

My guilt actually went down smoothly as I swallowed hard and offered, "Well, maybe it won't be so bad."

"Now that you're here, I'm sure it won't." Matt raked his hand through his thick mop of shiny hair, and I started to swoon until he added, "Having a friend around makes anything more bearable."

Matt thinks we're friends? Unless he's thinking Ross and Rachel, there's more work here than originally calculated.

"Okay, so like hand me some issues and we'll get started," I directed. "Since these quizzes are designed for girls but are about boys, what if I ask you some questions? Then we can make up our own list of more appropriate quiz topics. How does that sound?"

"Sounds fine, Cher. Like I said, I'm not really into this stuff, so ask away."

I flipped through some magazines and pretended to read. "Okay. Has anyone ever called you by another name?" I figured I'd dispense with the Matt-as-twins theory first.

Matt seemed suspicious. "Is this really part of the quiz?"

I nodded. "The how-well-do-you-know-him? part."

"Just Matthew." He shrugged. "It's what my mom used to yell when she was ticked."

"But she doesn't anymore?"

"No, she, uh . . . isn't usually that mad at me anymore."

I continued, "Is there someone in your family who looks like you?"

"Cher, let me see that," Matt said, reaching over to my desk. "If that's how they're telling girls to find out about guys, this whole thing reeks worse than I thought."

"I totally agree, Matt. Let's go to another issue," I said quickly, tossing the magazine I was pretending to read away and picking up another one. "Let's try this one: 'Love Chemistry: How to Find Out if He's Totally into You.'"

Matt rolled his eyes, but I plowed on. "It's true or false. Here's the first statement: 'Love chemistry can't be faked.'"

"True," he answered definitively, crossing his arms behind his head and leaning farther back in his chair. "You can't make yourself feel something for a girl just because your friends think she's hot. You either feel it yourself or you don't."

I smiled bewitchingly. "Next. 'Chemical reactions, like love at first sight, are always instantaneous.' "

Matt pursed his pillow-lips and got way thoughtful. Then he chose "False. It's like with a picture. You shoot something in one light, and you're like, yeah, this is okay. But then you shoot the same subject in another light, and she's . . . I mean, it's . . . it just takes your breath away. And it's like you react completely differently. Does that make any sense, Cher?"

"Sense *and* sensibility, Matt," I said admiringly. Then I dove headfirst into the awkward silence. "True or false: 'You are now, or have recently been, in love.' " Okay, so that one wasn't part of *Savvy*'s quiz, but I had to know. And if I had been scripting this scene? This would totally be the part where Matt leans tenderly over toward me, cups my face in his strong, gentle hands, gazes deeply into my eyes, and whispers, "Does right now count?"

Only it didn't go exactly that way. Instead, in a severe mood swing, Matt quipped, "Does my camera count?"

"Animate objects only," I responded.

"Then, uh, no, probably not. False."

Semi dope! He's not involved with another Betty but isn't ready to admit his obvious feelings for me. Matt's intense stare gave him away. He wasn't eyeballing his Nikon. His view-finder was aimed at me.

I took a deep breath. "Okay, let's continue. 'What do

you consider the most important element in a relationship: common interests, physical attraction, or timing?' "

"That's not a true or false question, Cher," Matt astutely pointed out. "But I'll answer you anyway. None of the above."

I closed the magazine. I had the distinct impression Matt knew I wasn't reading from it. I ventured, "So like, then, what *is* most important to you in a relationship?"

"Honesty, Cher. That's what. I consider honesty the most important aspect of any relationship." Matt's gaze shifted to the window and I followed it, but I couldn't see anything except patches of smog. He continued. "If two people can't be honest with each other, why bother? But that's the one thing most people avoid at any cost. I think for most of us, the most terrifying thing in the world is being completely honest."

"It's such a lonely word," I agreed sincerely. "But, Matt? Don't you also think that people express their true feelings in different ways? I mean like, not everyone can just blurt out what they're feeling. My best friend, De, and her boyfriend, Murray? They can never say what they're really feeling, so they fight all the time. It's their way of expressing their honest love for one another. Or take Shakespeare. Maybe he couldn't express his feelings for a Betty, so he wrote *Romeo and Juliet* instead. Does that make any sense, Matt?"

Matt's eyes totally lit up. Chronic! I'd touched on something close to his soul. "That's it! It's like you just said, Cher. Sense and sensibility. Take me. I might not always say what I'm feeling, but I express myself in my pictures. That's where my real feelings are exposed. That's why I could never do the kind of photography they do here. All that fashion and modeling stuff. It's so posed, so phony."

I hung on to Matt's every word. It was our deepest interface ever. Even if, on the topics of fashion, beauty, and models, I so disagreed. But Matt was furiously passionate, so I coaxed further. "So if you don't want to be the next Scavullo, then who is your freeze frame role model?"

"Weegee." Matt answered without blinking.

Matt idolized one of the Bee Gees? I knew they were famous for that disco stuff, but I'd never heard about photographic prowess. No, that couldn't be it. I had no clue what Matt was talking about, but I didn't want to seem photo-impaired, so I went with, "Does he have a studio in L.A.?"

Matt guffawed loudly. I blushed deeply. Then, between peals of laughter, he was all "I'm sorry, Cher. I didn't mean to laugh at you. But after what we just said, you, uh, could have been honest."

Matt had totally nailed my lame attempt at cover-up. But he was instantly forgiving. "It's okay Cher. Most people have never heard of him."

"Could I hear about him now?"

"You really want to? I mean, it might be boring if you're not into it."

"No, really, I want to hear all about Mr. Gee," I insisted enthusiastically.

Which set Matt off laughing again. "I'm sorry, Cher. You're cute. It's not Mr. Gee. His real name was Arthur Fellig, but he went by Weegee. He started out as a photojournalist who worked the crime beat for a newspaper. But he got sick of that stuff. He really wanted to photograph people in the act of just being themselves. His idea was to catch them off guard, in the midst of their lives, absorbed in their misfortunes or their happiness. And he did. It was like, in the click of a split second, he captured all the drama of people's lives."

"And he got famous doing that?" I wondered.

"Very. He ended up photographing Andy Warhol and President John F. Kennedy. His photographs made it to *Life* magazine and *Vogue*."

"*Vogue!*" I lit up. Finally, Matt had moved into my turf. "Are there any of his pictures in the current issue?"

"I doubt it, Cher. Weegee died in 1968. But there are books with his stuff. The most famous is *Naked City*."

I glanced out the window. Slices of afternoon sun had begun to streak through the smog over our own city, and suddenly, it was like, Click! There it is: brainstorm. Matt was frantically encyclopedic about his subject, just like the other experts we'd commissioned to tutor Murray. What if I could get Matt to instruct Murray in all things photographic? It could be a *Jeopardy!* category, after all. Besides, it might be my only shot at moving Matt and me out of the brutally constraining confines of *Savvy* magazine.

"Matt?" I began. "I have a prodigious favor to ask you."

"Shoot, Cher," Matt said tenderly.

So I explained about how keeping Murray in school with us was a majorly worthy cause and how he could totally help. Matt seemed moved at our plight, but at first, not enough.

"I don't know how much help I could really be, Cher. I'm still learning about a lot of things myself. Besides, I don't have a lot of free time these days. But I could recommend some books."

"Murray does better with interfaces," I explained. "He's got like a kind of a photographic memory when you teach him stuff verbally."

Matt wasn't convinced. I had to think fast and be my most alluring self.

"Okay, I'll tell you what. Just meet Murray, talk to him. My friends and I are getting together for dinner tomorrow night at Jerry's Deli. Come with us and then decide if you want to . . . I mean, if you can, help out. Okay?"

Matt softened. "I'll check on it, okay? I'll get back to you tomorrow at work."

Chapter 9

*T*his was so jammin'! Matt agreed to a quick bite with my t.b.'s and me. He promised to bring his camera and show Murray all the photo need-to-knows. And it wouldn't be like a date or anything, but once Matt and I had our first out-of-office experience? It would be all that whole different lighting concept. Like when one of his formerly "just okay" pictures transforms into one of those breath-taker-away jobs.

Since Matt appeared to be vehicularly challenged, I offered to pick him up at home, but he was all "No problem, Cher. I'll meet you there." Which prompted De to point out that either he's too proud to let a girl drive (gallant but fixable) or he doesn't want me to know where he lives (he really is in the Witness Protection Program).

Jerry's Deli, which has nothing to do with *Seinfeld*, is

a way famous L.A. landmark. Tourists flock there for bodacious sandwich ensembles and regional delicacies like borscht soup. Every table is accessorized with pickles, mustard, and relish. There's even a tacky souvenir stand where you can buy Jerry's Deli logo sweatshirts, caps, and menus. Celebrities go there to be incognito or if they're really, really hungry. You never know who could be at the table next to you— John Travolta or the proprietors of Travolta Tires, vacationing from New Jersey.

Waiting for Matt to join us, I was ensconced at a round table with Murray, Sean, De, and Amber, who were massively engaged in an exciting round of the Six Degrees game. That's when you take a celebrity and try to connect him or her to other stars in six steps or less. Usually, it's played with Kevin Bacon, but we were doing Calvin Klein. We considered it part of Murray's education process for *Jeopardy!*

Murray was going, "Connect Calvin Klein to that evil director dude, Tim Burton."

Amber was all "Excuse me, like where's the challenge? Tim Burton directed *Edward Scissorhands,* which starred Johnny Depp, who's living with Kate Moss. Do I really need to go on?"

"Okay, okay, too easy. Try this one. Andre Agassi."

De rolled her eyes. "Still too elemental, Murray. Anyone knows that the highly evolved Andre is marrying the vertically evolved Brooke Shields, who, hello, starred in those archival commercials—"

Just then Matt walked in. And totally nothing came between me and my skip-a-beat heart. It was pounding so loudly, like when the car next to yours is blasting Metallica and drowns out your No Doubt CD. I was sure everyone could hear it. But who could blame me? Matt was a total specimen of Baldwinian prime, wearing that lived-in leather jacket that had totally succumbed to his every cut, his black jeans, and a University of Nebraska T-Shirt.

I waved. "Matt! We're here." As the hottie of my dreams ambled over and mumbled, "Sorry I'm late, Cher," I could tell he was fully approving my butternut yellow suede camisole top and cotton cargo pants, both by Ralph Lauren.

"You're right on time," I contradicted. "We haven't even ordered yet."

"Yeah, that's 'cause Cher made everyone wait for you," Sean said tactlessly, extending his hand and introducing himself. I finished the intro honors. As we ordered our sandwiches, salads, and sodas, I tried to hide my jitters. I so wanted my t.b.'s to appreciate Matt and vice versa. I mean, once Matt and I completely hook up, he'll be part of our posse. So he had to fit in. Like when those Charles Jourdan suede shoes just have to fit because they're the only pair in the entire universe that will match the Galliano dress.

Except that doesn't mean they won't be uncomfortable. Which, when I thought about it later, was a fairly apt description of our abbreviated dinner with Matt. Not that we all didn't try. We fully committed to his comfort-level among strangers. Maybe too hard. De pressed for personal details, like, could we see any pictures he's taken? Matt hadn't brought any. Amber just pressed. And fawned. "I must have that jacket! It's *très* au courant retro. Where'd you get it?"

Matt was polite but oblivious to Amber's attempts at

impressing him. "I've had it for years. I can't even remember where I got it." He shrugged.

Murray and Sean spent a few minutes doing their version of polite but soon reverted to homeboys at the deli behavior. Which would have deteriorated into a pickle-toss contest had De not intervened with a decisive kick to her man's left shin.

Murray kicked into gear. He focused on Matt and was all "Thanks for agreeing to help me out. Cher says you're the man with the photo-op plan. And, you know, I'm kinda more familiar with bein' on the *other* side of the camera."

Sean took that as his cue to swing his arm around Murray's neck, and the two grinned broadly, pretending to pose for a picture. This time I kicked both of them.

If Matt thought they were decorum-impaired, he didn't show it. "No problem, Murray," he said, "but like I told Cher, I don't know how much help I can be."

"Oh, but he can!" I interrupted, boldly squeezing Matt's hand. "I mean, you can—be an immense help. Matt's going to be way famous one day, the next Weegee." I flashed a dazzling dental display in his direction. Which Matt totally picked up on and rewarded me with a dimpled dose of his. "Tell them about how Weegee captured the drama of people's lives and how he was in *Vogue.*"

Matt squirmed, but, sign! He didn't try to slip his hand away from mine. And he was way informative, too, on the subject of his idol and a bunch of others in his category. He even extracted his camera from his backpack and pointed out some tech stuff. I hoped he didn't catch on to Murray's faux bug-eyed interest, punctuated with the occasional, "You don't say" or "That's fascinating" or Sean's lame attempts to conceal his giggling.

On the other hand, maybe he did. Tragically, after about a half hour, Matt glanced at his watch. "Well, I've gotta go. It was nice meeting everyone. Hope I helped a little. Good luck, Murray." He got up, withdrew a ten-dollar bill from his pocket, and said, "This should cover me." Then he grabbed his backpack and started to leave.

"Wait, Matt," I said. "I'll walk you out."

"Uh, sure, okay, Cher." Matt was heading for the door when suddenly, something caught his eye and he stopped short. I followed his glance—to the souvenir stand? "Hang on a minute. I think I'll pick up a sweatshirt," he said.

It sort of puzzled me, since Matt didn't seem to be much of a logo promoter. But when he strode over to the souvenir counter and pointed out a white Jerry's Deli sweatshirt in size small, it hit me. "For your sister Monica?" I guessed.

Matt gave me an enigmatic how'd-you-know-that? look. But all he said was, "Yeah, I think she'll like that."

"She's lucky . . ." I began, although something in Matt's look told me otherwise, ". . . to have such a thoughtful big brother," I finished quietly.

"Yeah, well. See you tomorrow, Cher." With that, he disappeared into the smoggy night. I wondered how he was getting home.

When I returned to our table, De and Amber had gotten up. "We're fast-forwarding to the ladies' room, Cher, but we waited for you," De said.

Before I could respond, Sean interjected, "Oooh, I have to go to the little boys' room. Murray, would you keep me company?"

I rolled my eyes at Sean, grabbed my mini-tote, and followed my t.b.'s. As soon as the door closed behind us, I was all "Did I not warn you? Is he not mad cute?"

De agreed. "He's all that, but—"

"But? Hello, girlfriends, the only butt worth noting is—"

"What I mean is, Cher, except when he's talking about photography, he's furiously quiet."

I totally bristled. "Unlike motor-mouth Murray, you mean? Or the master of mile-a-minute moronics, Sean? Matt's not like them. Matt's more the embodiment of that quote 'Still waters run deep.'"

To which the formerly fawning Amber tossed in, "Excuse me, sometimes still waters are just shallow."

"Well, when it comes to shallow, I bow to your expertise, Amber," I retorted. "Besides, Matt's more than just a megababe hottie. He's brilliant, sensitive, ambitious, and heroic, and he's a total softie when it comes to his little sister. He even stopped to buy her a sweatshirt just now."

"Why would he do that?" Amber asked. It didn't surprise me that the queen of Me-First would not understand the concept of giving to someone else. But that's not what Amber was questioning. "I mean, if he lives here, why buy an overpriced for-tourists-only souvenir?"

I couldn't answer that, so I didn't.

Murray and Sean were massively engrossed trading one-ups as we approached our table. Which is why they didn't immediately see me. I can only assume that if they had, their barbs wouldn't have been directed at Matt.

"Yeah, and what was all that Wee Wee stuff he was spoutin'?" Sean spouted with a mouth full of coleslaw. "About some diminutive photographer?"

To which Murray rejoined, "Pee Wee? I thought he said Ouija, the board that foretells the future."

"No, no, check it, man. He meant Squeegee, like those guys who clean your windshield with them dirty wiper-things."

Murray was all, "You sure it wasn't wedgie? I get them all the time when my Calvins ride up."

Sean slapped the table. "Psych! Maybe he meant Kathie Lee's dude. Ain't she always goin' 'Weegel'"

"Way mature, guys," I interjected, making my presence known.

"We didn't mean to dog your boy-toy" was Murray's lame attempt at cover-up.

"You didn't mean for me to hear you, Murray. Whatever. But if photography comes up as a *Jeopardy!* category, tails you lose because you were too busy goofing off to pay attention to Matt," I sniffed.

"Stop trippin', Cher. You got what you wanted, a romantic night out of the office with camera-boy."

"Yeah, don't think we didn't notice that little game of handsies you and him had goin' on," Sean taunted.

Murray finished, "Besides, I'm down with the real categories they're going to ask. My brain is trained! An' we got as much chance of photography coming up as you do of actually sustaining a relationship with Matt."

Okay, so reverting to childish behavior is significantly below me. But I could not help myself. I grabbed the entire pickle container, flung it at Murray, and turned on my heel. "Roll the credits—I'm over. Is anyone else coming?"

Amber stayed behind, but Dionne rallied. Instead of leaving as she'd gotten there, with Murray, my main big seat-belted herself into my Jeep, where at once she offered up an atoning Galleria sidebar, accompanied by a stellar idea on the side. "While we're soothing your bruised feelings with a balmy acquisitive spree, why not pick up a gift for a loved one?"

"Way olive branchy, De." I acknowledged her peace offering. "I accept."

I was picturing a gift for Matt—using De's credit card, of course. A Coach camera case to replace his battered and bruised backpack?

But that wasn't exactly the concept De had in mind. "It's too early in the relationship. You yourself said he bails the minute it gets too personal. Why not follow his lead and pick up a trinket for sister. Maybe that's the freeway that leads to his heart, Cher."

"Righteous idea, De!"

Almost giddily, I swung into the parking lot of the Galleria. De and I did a major beeline for FAO Schwarz, where we completely reverted to our childhood Bettys and let the luxury toy aura wash all over us. I picked up a Tickle Me Elmo. "You think?" I asked De. But De was all "She's too old for that."

"I'm not," I said, tickling the furry red creature's belly. It rewarded me with a giggle.

De rolled her eyes and said, "Let's segue to another aisle. Matt's sister is probably in that stage where, like, everything is too babyish for her. Like any eleven-year-old, she'd probably rather ralph in public than be caught playing with dolls."

"Unless it's this," I said, plucking an appetizing item from the shelf. "Look, De, it's a Barbie Fashion Designer CD-ROM! Budding Donna Karans can design doll-size outfits on their computers and then print them out—on actual fabric, in color. Just add tape and Velcro and it's ready to wear for any Barbie. It even comes with its own catwalk! Why did they not have this when we were tots?"

"We were born too soon, Cher."

"Oh, De, we *have* to get it. What eleven-year-old on the planet would not totally die for this?"

I snagged one for Matt's sister, Monica. Then De ran back to get one for herself. Okay, so did I.

Later that night, when Josh called to check up on how I was surviving without my credit card, I was fully truthful. Mine *was* still in dry dock. We'd used De's for all our necessities, but I didn't tell him that.

The next day at work, I dashed to Let's Get Quizzical. Matt was already there, pounding away furiously at the computer.

"Hi, Matt, what are you doing?" I said playfully, peeking over his shoulder.

"Typing up a list of quiz ideas for that male point of view thing Yolanda asked for the other day."

"Well, not to interrupt or anything, but I just wanted to say how grateful we all were that you helped out last night. And to so apologize for Murray and Scan. They were just nervous."

"They were fine, Cher. You don't have to apologize for anything."

"So, how'd your sister like the sweatshirt? Did it fit?" I asked innocently.

There was something in Matt's body language that said, "Don't go there, Cher." But how could I not? So I plowed on. "Anyway? After dinner last night, De and I sort of ended up at the mall. And guess what? I kind of picked up something for Monica, too." I offered him the shopping bag I was carrying.

Matt stiffened. There was an edge to my hottie's voice I hadn't heard before. "You bought something for my sister? Why?"

"No real reason. Didn't you say Monica is about eleven or somewhere in that range?"

"So?" Matt was getting dangerously edgy.

"Well, I remembered when I was eleven, and my total favorite thing to do, aside from practicing signing my name to a credit card receipt, was to outfit Barbie in designer fashions. Well, hello, it's the nineties and like, what will they think of next? Barbie's gone digital!" I displayed my CD-ROM Barbie Fashion Designer gift and showed him how it worked. "Dope, huh?"

Only somehow Matt misinterpreted. Instead of agreeing with my dope description, he made me feel like one. He stared at me in a way he never had before. It's a borderline call, but if I had to chose a word to describe it? I could go with menacing. Matt totally erupted at me. "What are you doing, Cher? What would ever make you think my sister would need, or want, some ridiculous thing like this? You don't even know her! Do me a favor. Don't buy presents for her! Don't talk about her like you know her! You don't! You don't know me, you don't know anything!" Matt tossed Barbie back at me, bolted up from the computer, and stalked out of the cubicle.

A burning, upchucking sensation overtook me. My lips trembled, and I could feel my eye makeup start to smear. What—what had just happened here? Was this the same Matt who'd defended my coffee-getting honor? Who'd taken me under his wing and taught me all about slides and lighting and Weegee? Who'd held my hand—sort of—at dinner last night? What did I do to deserve being trashed? And to make him so harshly reject my present? It wasn't even for him. And call me mental, but isn't rejecting a present on someone else's behalf, like, the epitome of rude? True devastation knocked at my door, and I totally flung it wide open. I could not even bring myself to call De. Well, not right away anyway. A full ten minutes later, I went to the coffee machine phone and punched in her digits.

"It was way harsh, De." I swallowed hard so I wouldn't sob into the phone. "I can't believe it. Why would he do that?"

De was massively flummoxed. "Cher? I really hate to bring this up, but what if Amber was right? Maybe there's stuff about Matt you don't know. Maybe he *is* too hottie to handle."

Chapter 10

Normally, the company my misery loves most is Daddy. But Daddy's been ferociously occupado lately. His study door is closed most of the time. Since I know better than to disturb him when he's so majorly engrossed, I refrained from an actual interface regarding the Matt devastation. But I did conjure up a virtual one.

"How do we handle our problems in this household, Cher?" Daddy would have said.

"We break them down, Daddy," I would have answered.

"Okay, so what's the worst part of your problem with this boy, who, from what I can see, doesn't even deserve you." I'm pretty sure Daddy would have said that.

And then I would have explained to Daddy that not

only had I been rejected by my total potential soul mate, I had no clue why. I toyed with Daddy's possible responses: A) Serve him a verbal subpoena, demand an explanation. B) Reject him right back. Ignore any reconciliation attempts he makes. But after much mental cross-examination, I settled on C) Stop obsessing and put your energies into more positive, solution-oriented endeavors. It was the most Horowitzian of the choices.

Serendipitously, I had a judicious amount of positive stuff to endeavor. Murray, for one. The taping for the real *Jeopardy!* was, like, next week. The intense parade of experts we'd commissioned were rotating through the revolving doors of Murray's life right on schedule. Everyone from local celebs like our own Mr. Hall and Miss Geist, to Daddy's colleague Chris Darden, to Martha Stewart for that frisky foods category, and even Fergie, for tutoring in the dos and don'ts of British royalty. Oprah couldn't come, but she did send her trainer.

And at school? The entire faculty cooperated by having us phrase our answers in the form of a question. Mr. Hall even let Murray call him Alex. Our fellow students chipped in with random advice. Some guy named Anonymous taped a note to Murray's locker offering the mantra "I am large and in charge." Murray repeated it ad infinitum. Or nauseam. In spite of my bitter heartbreak, I was way inspired at how everyone unselfishly pitched in for Murray. It was frantically people-affirming. Even Josh, who kept calling to check up on my life without credit cards, and "stop calling her my girlfriend" Melanie graced us for a cameo strategy session.

I relied on total recall of those positive feelings when I reported to work at *Savvy*. I applied a foundation of my game face under my makeup to fully cover my psychic wounds from Matt. Besides that, I tried to avoid him. Immediately after my bout with hottie humiliation, I got Vikki to transfer me out of Let's Get Quizzical.

Vikki and I had bonded so fully that she did a total one-eighty from that first day when she scolded, "Interns don't tell us where they want to be." This time she offered up the way nurturing "Which department do you want to be in, Horowitz?"

I'd done a one-eighty, too. Instead of promoting my Fashion & Beauty expertise, I quietly answered, "The one that's furthest from Matt."

It turned out to be Celebrities. And as it also turned out? Matt asked to be shifted, too. He was back in his beloved Photography. Still, we crossed paths sporadically. It was way awkward. Matt averted his eyes, making no move toward the apology-laced reconciliation he so owed me. I kept my vow to focus on positive and productive—as well as on the three college hotties Josh had waiting in the wings. Another week and my bet would be won!

And, as Amber didn't fail to remind me, "It's not like you ever actually had Matt, Cher, so, excuse me, what exactly did you lose?"

Maybe Ambular was right, and I'd been deep in Denialville all this time.

"Oh, Cher, I've been looking for you." It was Christie, princess of the Manic Panic nail color juliettes. She'd come to rescue me from my plunge into pity city. At least that's what I thought until she jauntily declared, "It's your turn!"

"My turn to what, Christie?"

"Don't say I didn't warn you. The call's out for all interns to report immediately to the photo studio. It's Fashion Flops time. And"—she playfully touched my arm—"tag, you're it!"

Not even. "Christie, you can't be serious. No way am I participating in this heinous fraud, foisted upon an unsuspecting public."

"If you want to keep this job you are." I actually heard Vikki cracking her gum before I heard her voice. My mentress walked over to us, authority-figure clipboard in hand. "Fashion Flops is one of our most popular features, and we strongly encourage all interns to participate. Besides, it's fun. It's something you can tell your grandchildren about."

Correction. It's something Amber will gloat to her grandchildren about.

Christie was all, "Come on, Cher. We all pose. It's like a rite of passage."

"More like a wrong," I sniffed.

"Look, Horowitz, think of it this way," Vikki interjected. "Think of the great service you're doing for, let's see, how would you phrase it? The fashion-impaired? Isn't it just as important to demonstrate what not to do?"

If I'd been at my fighting best, I would have resisted. But my scene with Matt had woefully diminished my spirit, so, conceding defeat, I followed Vikki and Christie to the photo studio.

Had I known that Matt was one of the photographers involved, however, I would have mustered whatever spirit I had left and bailed. Of all the moments for *Savvy*'s photo staff to pick to allow Matt to actually shoot live models! It was beyond humiliation.

To my credit, I kept that game face thing going and ignored him, as I was handed a grievous dis-ensemble to put on. It was a floral miniskirt, only to be obscured by an amazonian backpack and worsened by clashing tights. Still, I tried for some semblance of pride as I posed against a backdrop of a faux street corner, so readers would be lulled into thinking I was just some style-impaired random *Savvy* had ambushed on the street.

My attempt at pride-salvage was viciously trashed when the stylist came over. "Could you push the sleeveless shirt higher on your shoulder and pretend your bra strap is showing?" Without waiting for an answer, she brutally did it for me. I sneaked a peek at Matt, who looked embarrassed. I felt ickier than ever.

In vain, I asked for that black rectangular box they insert over the hapless fashion victim's eyes to mask her identity. Vikki gently told me they add that later, on the computer.

For what seemed like an eternity—tragically, not Calvin's—we posed in one heinous outfit after another. Trousers that were either too loose or too tight, a bunch of tie-around-the-waist sweaters for those moments when you need to add ten pounds to your look(!). Christie, who actually seemed to be enjoying this, wore platform boots—with knee-highs sticking out! Another girl had to suffer the indignity of pretending to pick her teeth in public; yet another internette got to model a hair-don't that looked like a Dunkin' Donuts–inspired pyramid.

I couldn't help laughing at that one. And then all of a sudden, the strangest feeling came over me. The absurdity of what we were doing caught up with me, and hello, I fully succumbed to it. I got into the spirit, pointing and guffawing along with everyone else, and even cracked silly. When it was all over and we were dismissed, I realized, hello, I'd completely temporarily forgotten about Matt. I guess that famous saying, therapy comes in all shapes and sizes, is true.

If I'd still been a newbie, I would have assumed a stint in *Savvy*'s Celebrities department was all a revolving door of Leonardos, Antonios, Tysons, and Brads. But by now I was fully real-world-centric. I expected to be kept far away from any actual premium stars, and that I would mainly be fetching java for a troupe of C-list handlers. That's why I was surprised on only my second day in that rotation to be asked to fetch Brad himself.

The editor of the Celebrities section was the charmingly fidgety and vertically challenged Leggs McNeil. He totally worshipped all celebrities big and small and felt that presenting them in their most soul-baring light through the pages of *Savvy* was his calling. I learned all this the first day, since Leggs was a big time chatterbox. I also learned that he believed "Exclusives, scoops, and never-before-seen photos" were the reason for *Savvy*'s success. Leggs's spirits were significantly airborne because not only had he snared an impossible-to-get interview with Brad Bancroft, he also had in his possession a photo no other publication [...] been able to get. It was a slide of Brad at the counte[...] Tiffany's slipping a diamond engagement ring onto [...] appropriate finger of his girlfriend, model-actress [...] Larson.

"He keeps denying he's engaged," Leggs decl[...] triumphantly, "but now, he's going to have to c[...] clean, and *Savvy*'s readers will be the first to kno[...] and see." Leggs licked his lips in anticipation, ad[...] that his sources at Tiffany's had tipped him off tha[...] ring was a five-carat job that set Brad back big [...]

"What if they want to keep that romantic mo[...] private, and Brad still doesn't want to admit [...] asked. "Are you going to show him the phot[...] dence?"

Leggs looked shocked. "Show him my prized [...] Absolutely not! What if he walks out on the inte[...] No, that photo will be *Savvy*'s little secret. Brad v[...] it with the rest of our readers, when the issue h[...] stands."

"But isn't that, like, less than honest?" I wor[...]

"What's honesty got to do with it? This is sh[...] my dear." And then he added with a chuckle[...] come to the real world, Cher."

In spite of his behind-their-backs sneakiness[...] also believed in the concept of full-tilt coddle f[...] star he interviewed. Which is why he insis[...] sending not just an empty—albeit luxu[...] limousine to collect Brad for the interview, [...] with a representative from *Savvy* in it. "I don't [...] send interns for something this important," [...] nervously, "but I sense you're not our run-of-[...]

gofer, Cher. You have style, charisma, class. I trust my instincts, and they tell me, 'Leggs, send her. She'll rise to the occasion.' "

Which is how I found myself in the jump seat of a plush limo, directly across from Brad Bancroft. The minute I saw him, the overwhelming urge to call De seized me. But I didn't think that was what Leggs meant by rising to the occasion. Besides, I still didn't have a cell phone. Brad did, however. Around his sinewy neck was a StarTAC wearable cell phone, only the most important accessory of the year. I instantly knew what I was going to do the minute I got my credit cards back! Hello, had I not earned this?

Brad, who had totally earned his reigning title of Sexiest Man Alive, had brought another accessory: Julia Larson. His secret fiancée wasn't scheduled to be with him, but there she was, live and in person. So after I welcomed them to *Savvy's* limo and all, I judiciously averted my eyes in case they wanted to lock lips. Except I couldn't help sneaking a glance. Julia was all tumbleweed curls, long, lush eyelashes and collagen-accented pouty mouth. But something was missing: the ring. And call me mental, but something else, too: like, any sense of affection between them. It didn't take long to see why. Hollywood's Hottest Couple was deep into a ferocious quarrel. Just like De and Murray, except without the underlying devotion.

In contrast to her soft look, Julia was way hard-line, demanding, "Tell them that love scene is out or you won't do the movie! It's what we agreed on."

Brad sighed. I had the feeling this wasn't a new argument. "No, Julia, it's what *you* wanted. *I* never

118

agreed to it. That scene is an integral part of the movie. Without it, there's no plot."

"Plot, schmot. When did you ever care about plot before!" Julia folded her arms across her chest and continued her steely-eyed tirade. "Audiences will flock to anything you're in and the studio knows it. It doesn't have to have a believable story. Look at *Independence Day!*"

"Here's what I'm looking at, okay, Julia? I'm looking at growth. I'm looking at stretching. I'm over the hunk thing. They don't give Oscars to sex symbols!"

I was about to mention Daniel Day-Lewis until I remembered that technically, I wasn't part of this conversation. It raged on without me. We'd almost reached our destination when Julia threw down the gauntlet: "The movie with the love scene in, or me—out of your life. Choose, Brad."

But then the most amazing transformation happened. As soon as we got to *Savvy*'s offices, Brad and Julia acted as if nothing had happened. They were judiciously lovey-dovey. And Brad was massively professional as he ducked and darted around Leggs's questions about their relationship. No matter how much Leggs pressed—and he did everything short of shoving the engagement ring slide in their faces. For the record, neither Brad nor Julia would admit to being anything beyond "the greatest of personal friends" and having "the deepest respect for each other." I guess that's why they call it acting.

Later, in the photo studio, Brad posed sexily solo but nixed all requests for shots with Julia. She pretended to agree wholeheartedly with the decision. I could tell

Leggs was disappointed, but then again, he already had his ace in the hole: the engagement ring shot.

While I was psyched to be privy to the interview, I tried and failed to beg off accompanying Brad, Leggs, and Julia into *Savvy's* photo studio. I knew Matt would be there. Which he was, along with a slew of other photographers, stylists, assistants, and a smattering of interns who'd snuck into the shoot.

Matt saw me before I saw him. Instead of the guilt-ridden eye-aversion he'd been doing for the past few days, this time he focused squarely on me. He didn't say a word, and, okay, like I know this is completely mental, but I totally saw little swatches of remorse deep in his caramel eyes.

Chapter 11

*S*watches of remorse? What was I thinking? Hello, if Mr. "If two people can't be honest with each other, why bother?" was about to wake up and smell the apology he so owed me, he would have done it by now. After the Brad shoot—like, any time over the following few days—there had been massive opportunities for Matt to create a Kodak moment with me. But my ex-hottie didn't choose any of them. He reverted to Cher-avoidance. And while a part of me was still "I demand an explanation!" another part was like, And risk getting trashed again? I don't think so.

"Cher! Planet Hollywood to planet Horowitz, come in please!" I had no idea how long Leggs had been standing at my desk, leaning over me.

"My bad, Leggs. Did you need something?"

"It looks more like your *sad*, Cher. For a minute

there, you looked like Julia Ormond when Brad Pitt goes off to war in *Legends of the Fall.*"

I swallowed hard. Had my game face melted?

"I'll tell you what, sweetie. I'll commiserate with you—later. But first, it being Friday, we've got to offer up a sacrifice to the deadline deities. I just finished writing my exclusive feature on Brad Bancroft. It's got to go down to the art department stat. They're waiting for it. Here's the hard copy, here's the diskette—and here, Cher, are the slides to go with the layout. Including"—Leggs was soaring into the delight-o-sphere—"our little never-before-seen secret slide."

Leggs handed me all the materials for the story. The slides were packaged in that protective slide window sheet. I noticed the engagement ring shot was in the top row. I gripped it gingerly so it wouldn't fall out, as Matt had shown me in our halcyon days.

"Consider it delivered, Leggs," I said, bolting vertical from my seat, "And thanks for understanding."

"That's my girl. Chin up, Cher!"

I'd taken not two steps down the stairway toward the art department when I heard my name. "Horowitz!"

It could only be Vikki, calling out from her cubicle. I shifted into reverse and headed back up the stairs. Vikki's desk was majorly cluttered. If not for her carrot-colored hair, now glossy and relaxed thanks to my input, I barely would have seen her beneath the significant pile of paperwork. She was on the phone as two other lines flashed, demanding her attention. When she saw me, she was all "Horowitz! Great. You busy?"

"I'm on my way down to art with the Brad Bancroft story. They're going to press later today and they need it ASAP," I responded.

"Do me a giant-size favor?" Vikki implored. "Before you run downstairs, check the interoffice mail bin. I sent a memo to human resources and they never got it." She pointed to one of the flashing lines on her phone. "They're driving me crazy. They needed it yesterday. It's in a manila envelope that's clearly marked from me to human resources. Just pull it out of the interoffice mail bin, and after you've handed in the Brad story to art, fly by human resources and deliver it. Okay?"

"No problem, Vikki." I segued to the interoffice mail bin and flipped through a few envelopes in search of Vikki's missing missive. And then I saw it. Just as she'd described, it was from her, going to human resources. She'd marked it Personal & Confidential.

Okay, so later on? When I'd think about what happened next? I had to let myself off the hook. Like if they wanted stuff to really be confidential, why use those manila envelopes with the huge see-through holes in them for interoffice communiques? How could I help but see Matt's name peeking through one of those holes? This was a personal and confidential memo about Matt.

My heart raced. My conscience split in two and clashed. It was suddenly like *I* was the twins. The play-by-the-rules Cher said, "Don't open it. It says Confidential for a reason." The evil twin, hello, the *curious* twin—in a brutally need-to-know manner—was all "Are you mental? Open it! NOW!"

So like, okay, guess which Cher won out? But, your honor, like in my defense and all? My intentions were massively benign. I was all, I'll scan it, seal it back up, deliver it to its proper destination. No one gets hurt.

Subterfuge is so not my normal modus operandi, but it's not as if I've never seen a spy movie. I knew, like, I couldn't just stand in the middle of the floor and eyeball this highly confidential memo. I had to find some place inconspicuous, where I had no chance of being discovered. I headed for the coffee machine area, but it was riddled with java-fetching interns. I went to the ladies' room, but it was occupado. I trolled the entire editorial floor, scanning for random uninhabited cubicles, but grievously, no one had taken a sick day today. I was about to sneak out to the parking garage when it hit me. All the time Matt and I had been in Let's Get Quizzical, that editor Yolanda someone-or-other, had never made an appearance. Would she break form today?

She wouldn't. Her spacious cubicle was vacant. My heart pounded as I sat down quietly at her desk and carefully opened the memo.

On *Savvy* stationery, it was frantically official.

To: Human Resources, *Savvy* Publications
From: V. Nathanson, Intern Coordinator
Re: Matthew Rossman

I was pretty sure the next thing I read was a typo, because it had Matt's address—not even in the Valley. It listed his permanent residence as somewhere in

Nebraska? Which is like the Valley equivalent of the fifty states. I read on.

Status: Temporary
Evaluation & Recommendations: This intern will be leaving our program next week, therefore I am forwarding this evaluation for your files.

The memo went on to pinpoint Matt's radically fine points, including his stellar attendance record, conscientious attention to detail, willingness to tackle menial chores, and of course, his brilliance in the photo department. It even included a notation from Ms. Let's Get Quizzical on the golden quiz ideas he'd come up with during his brief rotation in her department.

And then it came. The paragraph I will remember forever. I fully committed it to memory:

You will note that this intern was folded into the program at the behest of the Family Support Center of Cedars-Sinai Medical Center, where intern's sister, Monica Rossman, is currently undergoing treatment for a life-threatening condition, the exact nature of which has not been disclosed to this company.

Therefore, the length of this intern's tenure had not been previously set, being based on his sister's progress. However, Dr. Armstrong has informed us that treatment is complete and the family will return to Nebraska. Please send a copy of this to Matt Rossman's high school (I believe you have that name and address on file) and instruct accounting to cut his final pay-check.

I was shaking as I resealed the memo and shoved it under Leggs's Brad story, which I was still carrying. So that's why there were pools of sadness in Matt's eyes whenever the topic of Monica came up. I had not misread them. I felt myself sliding into a deeply icky pool of my own sadness. What a duh-head I'd been! No wonder Matt had kept his distance. No wonder he went ballistic when I'd brought that gift to his sister. Like what good is a digital Barbie to someone who's fighting for her life? I had to find Matt and tell him. But tell him what? That I'd opened a confidential memo? That I'd not only gone behind his back, I'd gone behind Vikki's, too? If he'd wanted me to know, would he not have told me himself?

I had to call De. I used the phone on the still-AWOL Yolanda's desk.

De was all, "This is beyond tow-up, Cher. But I so bow to your powers of perception. You knew all along something was unkosher in Matt-land."

"What should I do, De? I have to tell him."

"As if! Cher, how can you? He'll be nuclear. And, I have to tell you, Cher, even though you're my premi-um t.b., he'd be justified."

Suddenly, out of nowhere, the sound of furiously cracking gum was upon me. "There you are, Horo-witz!"

Guiltily, I slammed down the phone, making sure, at the same time, that the confidential memo was ob-scured by Leggs's material for the Brad story.

126

But Vikki didn't notice that little maneuver. She was into an arduous tirade.

"An all-points bulletin has been issued for your whereabouts! You were supposed to deliver that story and those slides a half hour ago! And what happened to my memo? Human resources said they still don't have it! This isn't like you, Horowitz."

"I—I—had an emergency—sidebar," I stammered, heavy with the weight of my wholly unauthorized shocking discovery.

Vikki was close to postal. "Get everything down to art immediately! Go! Then deliver the memo to human resources. If I wasn't in the middle of twelve other crises, I'd do it myself."

As fast as my chunky platforms could take me, I rushed down the steps to the art department and handed over all the Brad materials to Jim. I turned on my heel to sprint to human resources, when I heard Jim call out, "Yo! Intern-girl! Come back. There's a slide missing."

Not even. "Not possible," I responded, bounding back to his desk.

"Possible," he shot back, holding the entire slide sheet up to the light to examine it carefully. "In fact, more like probable. Where's that shot of Brad and Julia that Leggs has been screaming about for the past week? It was supposed to be with the rest of this stuff."

In a move wholly inappropriate for an intern, I swiped the slide sheet out of Jim's hands. "Hello, it's right here, in the top—"

But it wasn't. The little windowette that previously housed the all-important engagement ring slide was vacant. I knew it was a stretch, but I went for, "So, like, okay, Jim. I'm totally not up for games. I've just had a majorly traumatic moment. So if you removed it and are trying to freak me out, you've succeeded beyond your wildest dreams."

Laid-back Jim had been replaced by going-on-ballistic Jim. "Look, Cher, I don't care what your personal trauma-rama is today. This is serious. This is the real world. Where's the slide?"

My heart lurched. Jim wasn't joking.

"It—it must have slipped out," I managed lamely. "I'll find it."

"You do that, Cher. Fast. I'll wait till I hear from you before I call Leggs."

Even though I knew I was about to trash my satin Versace hiphuggers I got down on my hands and knees and eyeballed the entire floor area from Jim's desk all the way back to the staircase I'd just flown down. I left no thread of carpet unturned. While I discovered a massive amount of dust and some crumpled yellow stickies, I did not find the slide.

I started to hyperventilate. At that moment, Manic Panic was no longer just the name of a nail polish company: It was me. For the second time in less than a week, I conjured up Daddy's voice. It said, "In moments like this, what do we do, Cher?"

I took deep, calming breaths. I don't know if I said it out loud, but the words "Retrace your steps, Cher. Slowly. Carefully. Meticulously" resounded in my ears.

I was the poster child of meticulosity as I retraced every step. I did a thorough search of Yolanda's cubicle first. Then I checked the coffee area. I ducked into the ladies' room. I trolled the entire editorial floor, my eyes riveted to the floor. Tragically, no runaway slide revealed itself. I was on my way back to Yolanda's office for a do-over, when I turned a corner and ran smack into . . .

"Matt!"

"Cher? What's the matter? You look . . . weird."

Matt looked weird, too. Alarmed almost.

"Matt, I—I—" My heart was on the palpitation express. I gulped. "I did something colossally bad. Actually? Square that. I did two colossally bad things."

"What happened, Cher?"

I locked eyes with Matt. All traces of his former wigged-out feelings had vanished. I saw only brutal concern. My instinct was just to tell him about the missing Brad slide, but when I looked into his eyes, I remembered what he'd said about honesty. I felt I owed him the knowledge of what I now knew.

"Matt, I'm beyond frenzied, but can we talk?" I pulled him into Yolanda's still empty office. I sucked in my breath. And like, a major confession-session toppled out. "You know what you said about brutal honesty? About how it's the most terrifying thing for most people? And about Weegee?"

Matt braced himself on the corner of Yolanda's desk.

I told him about the memo.

"So now you know." It was a statement. Like, "The End." He straightened up and started to leave.

I took a giant step after him. "Matt, wait. Why didn't you tell me? I would have understood. You could have leaned on me."

Matt paused. It took a while, but then, he seemed to come to a momentous decision. Slowly, he turned back, dropped into a chair, and exhaled deeply.

"I don't know, Cher. It's not like I was sworn to secrecy or anything, not really. I guess . . . I don't know if you can understand this, but I kind of made this weird pact with myself. It was like, as long as I don't say anything to anyone, Monica will get better. I know it's nuts. Telling anyone wouldn't have changed a thing. Does this make any sense to you at all?"

Only ultimate sense. It was like when Josh and I were racing to the non-earthquake event. I made that imaginary pact with the milk mustache billboard, like "If Daddy's okay, I'll drink more milk." I so deeply understood.

Matt continued. "And, anyway, it's kind of private. It's a family thing. Blabbing to people about Monica just felt like betrayal."

"You thought I would betray you?" I whispered.

"Or feel sorry for me, I don't know. You're such a cool girl. Probably the coolest I ever met."

"I am?"

Tragically, Matt didn't keep going on that trajectory. He was all "It just got so complicated. When I realized I liked you, I didn't know what to do. I knew I'd be leaving. But the worst of it was when you came with that doll present. It was the day of Monica's surgery, and I was an emotional wreck. I wanted to be at the hospital, but my parents made me come here after school. They said it was better for me. Like being here was going to keep me from worrying about it!"

I drew close to Matt and took his hands in mine.

He whispered, "I knew it was wrong to take out my frustrations on you. And then I didn't know how to apologize. And the more time that went by . . . it just got harder." When Matt looked up at me, I totally melted.

"Matt, I feel like such a tard. The way you reacted was beyond understandable." I wanted to console him, but suddenly, I heard voices coming from down the hall. They jolted me back to reality.

"Matt, there's something else I need to tell you. I'm in furious trouble."

"Can I help, Cher? I'll do anything."

I gulped. "Remember the one thing you said to never, ever do? I kind of did it. I kind of lost *the* slide. It was in that top windowette of the slide protector sheet, and it must have slipped out."

I half expected Matt to join the chorus of ballistics experts and go off on me, but he was awesomely supportive.

"We'll find it together, Cher. Come on, let's retrace your steps, exactly from the moment Leggs handed it to you. Let me call down to Jim first, in case he found it and you don't even know it."

Jim hadn't, but he did agree to give us more time before he Shawshanked me.

Together Matt and I traced. And retraced. We tracked. And backtracked. We scanned, we fine-tooth-combed, we were on a full search-and-retrieve mission. But the Brad and Julia engagement ring photo outsmarted us: it remained MIA. I half wondered if Brad himself hadn't sneaked back in the office and snatched it from me.

"I have to tell Leggs," I finally conceded. "He'll be so disappointed." Like matzo in the desert, I totally didn't rise, for any occasion. Instead, I went all flat and squashed his exclusive.

"Don't tell him," Matt said decisively. "Tell Vikki. She's responsible for us. Let's let her take it from here."

Vikki! As if what I'd done wasn't obtuse enough, I suddenly remembered that I still hadn't delivered her memo! I bolted. "Let me run this over to human resources, Matt, and then I'll tell her."

Matt was all courage under fire. "We'll tell her together, Cher. I'll be right by your side."

Vikki was stunned. And I even omitted the part about what exactly had distracted me and caused me to lose the slide. Matt said there were bounds to honesty, and Vikki didn't really need to know that I'd opened the memo.

But when she recovered from being stunned, a total weird thing happened. She morphed into furious businessy behavior and immediately jumped to, like, priority one. She called Jim in the art department first. They agreed to find out if anyone had thought to make a copy of the missing slide and then to a fall-back plan in case no one had. If they had no other options, they'd have to work with Leggs and redo the layout.

Vikki was all "This magazine has to go to press, kiddies, and it will, with or without that slide. Now, Horowitz? Rossman? Go home. I'll handle everything from here."

"But how can we leave you in your time of need, Vikki?" I asked anxiously.

Vikki was more exasperated than postal when she said, "I think you've done quite enough, thank you. Just go, okay? And, Horowitz? Wait until you hear from me before coming back to work on Monday, you know?"

Chapter 12

*I*t was all that famous poem about "It was the best of times, it was the worst timing ever." I'd finally uncovered Matt's poignant secret, and the truth had brought us the freedom to be together. Only we couldn't be, because I grounded myself for the weekend as punishment for screwing up so massively at *Savvy*. I retreated to my Laura Ashley–inspired barracks: that is, my bedroom. But being a lawyer's daughter, I know the Shawshank rules. I allowed myself one phone call. It was to Matt, and it marathoned all weekend. We had so much filling-in-the-blanks to do. And time was so not on our side.

During the course of our phone-fest, Matt fully explained everything. Monica was in L.A. for a kidney transplant. But because there'd been complications, her surgery was furiously delicate. After prodigious research, Matt's parents had chosen Cedars-Sinai Medical Center, since it was A-list for that kind of operation. Matt's family had moved to Los Angeles temporarily, so they could be together during their arduous plight.

"The hospital has a support system for the families of the patients, especially if they've had to relocate for a time," Matt explained. "They helped my dad work out something with his job. They got me placed at a local high school, and they found me this job at *Savvy*."

"What kind of job do you have at home?" I wondered.

"I don't have one. Just like you, Cher, this was my first. The expenses for Monica's surgery are astronomical, and our health insurance only goes so far. It's a struggle for the whole family. I just figured, you know, if I could at least handle my own expenses, it would help a little."

"The surgery's over, right? How's Monica doing?" I crossed my fingers, hoping for good news.

"We won't know for sure for a few months," Matt admitted ruefully, "but so far, it looks promising. She's recovered enough for us . . . Well, she'll be released from the hospital by the middle of next week."

"Stellar!" I was psyched for Matt's family, even though I knew that it meant that my hottie's return to the hinterlands was imminent. He knew it, too, but we didn't dwell on it. We talked about his car—hello, he did so have one, only he had to leave it at home. We talked about how he missed his friends, how he even missed his mom calling him Matthew. "She's too involved with Monica to pay much attention to me," Matt allowed. But we covered upbeat topics, too. Our favorite movies, videos, CDs. And like, memo to Amber: it's briefs, not boxers.

Our conversation circled back to Matt's volcanic explosion at me. He was rampantly remorseful. I'd fully commuted his sentence, but he couldn't forgive himself. He was all "I was so uptight. I thought Monica might . . . you know, never get to play with that doll. I was really evil to you. Can you ever forgive me?"

Just then my call waiting beeped. While I'd only allowed myself one call, something told me, Cher, bend the rules and answer this. I was massively grateful I did, because it was De—with a chronic news flash. "Cher! Quick! Turn on Channel Seven! *Entertainment Tonight* is on. Brad and Julia broke up! There's an in-depth report!"

I got back on the line with Matt, and we agreed to suspend conversation to devote our full attention to the earth-shattering this-just-in.

The Barbie doll of anchor-babes, Mary Hart, was all "So this looks like the end of the road for the romance of Brad Bancroft and Julia Larson. But you have to give them credit for scooping the tabloids and making the announcement themselves. The couple gave no reason for the break-up."

Too bad they hadn't called me for comment. Brad obviously chose that stretching, growing, and going-for-the-Oscar thing over Julia.

Mary continued. "Hollywood's formerly hottest couple did admit they had been close to getting engaged. In fact, they even shopped for rings but never bought any. Their statement ends this way: 'We continue to have the utmost respect for each other and intend to remain the best of friends.' "

Then Mary turned to the Ken-doll of news anchors, Bob Goen, and said, "Well, I hate to say it, Bob, but there's going to be a lot of celebrating by single women all over the country tonight."

Starting with . . . Cher Horowitz! I grabbed the phone. "This is so choice! Oh, Matt, that photo was faux! They might have been in Tiffany's, but they never bought a ring. Leggs's story was based on a faux assumption."

Matt rode my wave length. "Just think. If you hadn't lost that slide, Cher, how stupid *Savvy* would look coming out with not only dated but false information." Matt and I continued our celebratory conversation, until he drastically veered back to the course he was on before De's jubilant interruption.

"You know, Cher, you still didn't answer my question. What can I do to make it up to you for being such a jerk?"

"Well, for one thing, you can give Monica my present now," I quipped.

"You know it! And something tells me she's going to love it."

"And for another?"

"Name it, Cher."

"Come with us to the *Jeopardy!* taping. It's Monday, and Murray's going to need all the support he can get. They even declared a school hiatus so we could all be there for him."

Matt didn't answer instantaneously, so I added, "If

anyone knows what it's like to be wrenched away from friends, you do. It could happen to Murray."

That did it. Matt was all "I'll be there, Cher. But, uh, can you pick me up?" And then Matt said the words I'd waited nearly thirty grueling days to hear.

"Cher? One other thing. Once, before I leave to go back home, will you go out with me?"

My t.b.'s and I agreed to meet at the entrance to Sony Studios, where *Jeopardy!* is taped. As Matt and I pulled into the parking lot, we hooked up with our contingent, which included Murray, De, Amber, and Sean—his hair today a fetching rainbow sherbet confection from his Rodman kit—assorted members of the Crew, plus other randoms I pegged as *Jeopardy!* groupies. The adult faction was represented by Mr. Hall, Miss Geist, and Murray's parents.

Although we were all appropriately attired, Murray was top shelf. He'd done an unexpected but frantically appropriate mix of Perry Ellis conservative and trendy Nautica. It said respectful yet real. De was totally swooning. When they had to separate—Murray was directed to the contestant waiting room, we were sent to the audience seating area—De fully doused her man with a luxurious parting lip lock.

Amber doused him with some parting gift advice. "Relax, Murray. Just be yourself. On second thought, if you are being yourself? Be someone else."

It reminded me of that famous poem, "Beautician, heal thyself."

While *Jeopardy!* prided itself on that lavish new set, they'd opted for bargain basement in the audience seating department. Our accommodations were furiously bleacher-like. On the up side, we had scored the front row and our view of the stage was luxe. There was a barricade in front of us, but as if they had a premonition we'd be jumping over it, it was only knee high.

We'd barely settled on the seating arrangements when we heard *Jeopardy!*'s familiar, if normally disembodied, voice-over announcer, Johnny Gilbert, bellowing, "This . . . is . . . *Jeopardy!* Now entering the studio are our three Teen Tournament contestants. . . ."

A pert brunette in a Gap sweater and A-line skirt strode in and confidently took her position behind lectern number one. ". . . A senior from Huntington Beach High School, Katherine Flanagan!"

Katherine's contingent, seated behind us, applauded enthusiastically. De started to trash her French tips, stage-whispering, "Cher! It's a Flanagan! What if she's directly related to the one who beat Josh?"

The announcer continued. "Next, a senior from the Brentwood Academy in Locust Hills, Daniel Boylan." Daniel had that impossible prep-school pale geek aura. So did his entire cheering section, who were all decked out in identical school uniforms. I was tempted to corral their leader to talk color schemes but held myself back.

"And from Bronson Alcott High School in Beverly Hills, Murray . . ."

Sean completely drowned out the rest of Murray's introduction, yelling at the top of his lungs, "Give it up for Murray!" And, "Murray! Murray! He's our bro! If he can't do it, y'all don't wanna know!"

Which prompted all of us, including Murray's parents, to get into the spirit making up random cheers, until a page—*Jeopardy*'s version of an intern—came over and brutally shushed us.

We quieted down just in time to hear, "And now, the host of *Jeopardy!*, Alex Trebek!" No offense to AT, but his cheering section lacked our enthusiasm. The screen behind Alex immediately began making those twinkling sounds when they uncover the categories. De gasped as each one unfurled. They were Singularly Named Stars; Shakespeare; Planes, Trains & Automobiles; Let's Visit Liechtenstein; Legal Eagles; and— Amber totally went slack-jawed—Greasy Foods.

Alex instructed Murray to pick first.

But instead of, "I'll take Shakespeare for one hundred dollars," Murray flashed a bodacious grin and went, "Yo, Alex, my man, before we begin? I'd just like to say hey to my woman. De, baby! You are all that!" De responded by giggling and blowing kisses in Murray's direction.

Alex seemed immune to Murray's touching salute. The encyclopedic host repeated that Murray should pick a category. Flashing another goofy grin, Murray covered his eyes with one hand, pointed to the screen with the other, and went, "Eeny, meeny, miney, mo—"

"Murray!" Oops, Alex was getting testy now.

Murray got with the program. "I'll take Planes, Trains, and Automobiles for three hundred dollars."

Leave it to Murray to start large.

Alex read the clue: "The Monkees took it to number one."

Okay, so Murray might've started large? But he hadn't quite nailed "in charge." Alex called on Katherine, insinuating that she'd buzzed in first. Katie came through with the rampantly correct, "What is 'The Last Train to Clarksville'?"

De was frustrated. "He knew that one!"

"Simmer, girlfriend. He's got the whole board to conquer."

The board got conquered, all right, only not by Murray. It was way whiplashy, as Daniel and Katherine Ping-Ponged what-is-ing through the categories. And it's not like Murray didn't know the answers. His frantic attempts to ring in were heart-wrenchingly obvious. But Murray was buzzer-betrayed. As the round went on, it was like, Katherine: $1200; Daniel: $1400; Murray, "on the board with $0."

We had to do something. The minute they broke for a commercial, De, Sean, and I broke ranks, jumped the barricade, and dashed up to Murray. We made him take deep calming breaths. We made the *Jeopardy!* gnomes replace his buzzer, just in case. We made Sean shut up when he suggested "silencing" Daniel and Katherine.

When they resumed play, to our immense relief Murray got in the buzzer groove and majorly flourished. He buzzed in first and correctly with the answer to the clue, "It left at the stroke of twelve," by proffering, "What is 'The Midnight Train to Georgia'?"

Daniel kept pace with his thorough knowledge of Legal Eagles, though he did mix up F. Scott Fitzgerald and F. Lee Bailey. And who would've taken Katherine for a Liechtenstein connoisseur?

Murray furiously rebounded on Greasy Foods, with pretty much a rundown of his weekly diet, "What is . . . French fries?" "What is . . . ribs?" "What is . . . croissants?" "What is . . . potato chips?" "What is . . . KFC?" Murray was racking up dollars like Amber racked up heinous ensembles.

Murray chose Singularly Named Stars next. The controversy that erupted was titanic. The clue was, "He drives around Minneapolis in a little red Corvette."

Murray buzzed in first. When Alex acknowledged him, Murray flashed his dental accessories, and said, "Who is . . . ?" followed by the sound of silence. Alex assumed Murray had choked, deducted the money from his total, and went to Daniel, who was all, "Who is the Artist Formerly Known as Prince." They had to stop tape when Murray went ballistic, arguing that Prince's new name was that unpronounceable sign and therefore, he was correct in remaining silent. The controversy raged on for minutes. It resolved with Murray getting his money back, but woefully, Daniel got to keep his.

By the Double *Jeopardy!* round, the scores were close to even. The new categories unveiled were British Royalty; Proverbs; Food; Catching Some Z's; Jim Carrey Movies—I checked Amber's pulse when they announced that one, because I was pretty sure she had none—and the whimsical Pliny the Elder. Okay, so it's not whimsical. Leave it to Katherine-the-know-it-all to know Pliny was an ancient, furiously quotable Roman scholar.

But thanks to Fergie's tutoring, Murray totally knew the difference between the Queen Mum and the Queen, though Fergie had expressed negativity toward both. He only slipped up once. In response to "This future monarch is a teen idol," Murray said, "Prince William."

There was a split second of silence, broken when Sean shouted, "You forgot to say 'What it is'! I mean, 'What is'!"

Tragically, it was too late. Katherine buzzed in with the smug, "Who is Prince William, Alex." A page threatened to eject Sean.

When it was Murray's turn again, he hit pay dirt. Or should have. He opted for the tricky Proverbs, for one thousand dollars. It was the Daily Double.

"How much do you want to wager, Murray?" Alex asked.

De and I gripped our seats. We needed no psychic hotline to know what Murray was going to do. Was he not, after all, Murray? The words tumbled out. "I'll risk it all, Alex."

"A courageous move," Alex noted. "If you're right, you jump into the lead. If you're wrong . . ."

It was like everything fell into slow motion. Alex unveiled the proverbial clue. "In the land of the blind, this man is king."

We saw Murray's grin widen as Alex enunciated each word. And I can't be sure, but I think Mr. Hall gave Miss Geist smelling salts when Murray broke out with, "Alex, he has *left* the building! Who is . . . Elvis!"

The screen where Murray's total should have been was wiped clean. Alex was all "No, Murray, I'm sorry. The correct response was, 'Who is the one-eyed man.'"

Luckily, they had to stop tape for a technical

problem, so De and I broke for the stage, waving our arms frantically and calling, "Sidebar! Sidebar!"

A security guard tried to body block us with a dire warning. "Stop! You got away with this once, but not again! Return to your seats."

"But we need a sidebar!" I implored.

"This is not a trial! We don't have sidebars here. This is—"

De was all "Yeah, yeah, we know. This . . . is . . . *Jeopardy!* But my man's in real jeopardy! He needs us to get his groove back."

The *Jeopardy!* police radioed for backups and brutally threatened expulsion if we didn't retreat, like, immediately. We settled for flashing sign language at Murray, which must have done the trick, because he did get back on track. At least he swept his mothership category, Jim Carrey movies.

It wasn't enough to match Katherine's and Daniel's totals, though. As they broke for the last commercial, Alex reminded him, "You're still on the board, Murray, so you're eligible for *Final Jeopardy!*"

But when they revealed that final do-or-die category, my heart skipped a beat. It was Famous Photographers. I turned to Matt. We all turned to Matt. Then Alex intoned, "Here's the clue. You have thirty seconds to write your questions."

The board unveiled these words. "Famous candid photographer whose signature snapshots caught his subjects unawares. His portraits of Andy Warhol and John F. Kennedy appeared in *Life* Magazine."

The *Jeopardy!* theme music played as I pursed my lips and gripped the seat. Murray seemed to be writing frantically. Finally, after "What is the longest thirty

Jeopardy! mosh pit. Only Matt and I stayed in ou
seats. Our own little universe.

The celebration continued in the parking lot, whic
Murray's parents had efficiently turned into a lavis
tailgate party, with catering by Subway, which wa
next door to the studios. Sean's spirits had hardly bee
dented by his brutal ejection. He ran around th
parking lot waving his arms in the air, yelling tha
classic line from the movie *Jerry Maguire,* "Show m
the money! Show me the money!"

Murray's winnings were on Amber's mind, too, a
she coltishly advanced on our conquering hero. "S
Murray," she purred, although to the untrained ear
sounded more predatory. "All that newfound moola
Going to invest it? Share a stock tip with your woman -
best friend?"

Murray went faux casual. "Haven't decided ye
Amber."

But Murray wasn't being honest. In fact, he ha
decided. As he later told me, when we ducked behind
minivan for privacy, "As soon as that category cam
up on the board for *Final Jeopardy!* I knew what I'd d
if I won. I'm donating all the money to help with Matt'
sister's medical bills."

"Murray!" I threw my arms around him and buried
my face in his Perry Ellis shirt as the tears welled
up and threatened to trash my makeup. "That is
so—"

But Murray refused to accept any emotional props.
"Yo, Cher, it's only right. The way I see it? That dough
belongs to your camera boy, not to me. If it weren't for
him, I could've written Allen Funt, too!"

Murray swore me to secrecy. "I gotta do this anonymously, Cher. I might not have anything in common with Matt, except we're both men. And real men don't do embarrassed. So let's keep this one among friends."

I sniffed, "We'll keep it real, Murray. I promise. He'll never know."

Chapter 13

*I*t usually takes prodigious shopping, Polaroid-snapping, and several trips through my live-in closet to prepare adequately for a date, even for a Wednesday night. But I already knew what I was going to wear from the moment Matt asked me out: the midnight blue velvet overalls I'd worn to *Savvy* the day Matt said, "Wow, you look great." I don't normally do retreads, but the effect of my glowing blond highlights bouncing off the midnight blue overall straps would be stellar.

It *was* stellar. Like that famous sports poem, it was all "nothing but net," from the moment I drove to Matt's family's temporary digs in Burbank to pick him up. I got to meet his family, even Monica, who was a pint-size, feminine version of Matt. The whole family was in stratospheric spirits because they'd just gotten awesome news. Monica's test results had come back, and as of now, it looked like the transplant was going to be successful. Her body had not rejected anything. She didn't reject my digital Barbie, either, but had the same giddy appreciation for it as De and I had when we'd first discovered it. I even sat down on Monica's bed and gave her a few wardrobe tips to get her started.

Then Matt and I climbed into my Jeep and fully appreciated each other. I thoroughly thumbs-upped his choice of an Eddie Bauer–inspired sports jacket and denim shirt tucked into Abercrombie & Fitch khakis.

"Your skin is as soft as your overalls," Matt murmured, leaning over to stroke my cheek. I responded by brushing that adorable runaway lock of hair back and planting a smoochie on his cheek.

"So where should we go, Cher? A movie? Dinner?"

Since Matt and his family were leaving viciously early the next morning to return to Nebraska, our date could only span a few hours. And since it was our first and possibly only date ever—like, waste it on a movie, where we couldn't talk? Or in a restaurant, surrounded by randoms? As if!

"Have you ever been up to Mulholland Drive?" I asked.

Mulholland Drive is furiously famous. It's a curvy road that coasts along the peaks of the Hollywood Hills, all the way to the highest spot in L.A. It's way Mason-Dixony, the dividing line between L.A. and the Valley. On a low smog-alert night, you can see all the entire valley below you on one side and maybe, after skipping over a few states, even as far as Nebraska on the other. The road architects thoughtfully carved out parking pit stops all along the precipice, making Mulholland Drive one of the primo romantic settings in the world.

When we reached our cruising altitude spot, I found a place to park and we got out of the car. I perched on a rocky ledge and gazed down. The lights of the valley sparkled like a string of pearls against the neck of night. Matt stood behind me and encircled me with his furiously able arms.

"Isn't the view, like, luminous?" I said.

Matt nuzzled my neck. "You're what's luminous, Cher."

I whirled around because I suddenly remembered the CD I'd brought.

"Hold that thought, Matt." I dashed over to the parked Jeep, turned on the motor, and hit the CD player power button.

"Do you want to dance?" I asked coyly, meandering back to Matt.

Matt seemed surprised until the music started. It was *The Lion King* soundtrack. The song I'd chosen fully expressed my feelings. It was, "Can You Feel the Love Tonight?" We could. Totally.

When the song finished, Matt pulled away from me and shyly said, "I have something for you, Cher." He withdrew an envelope from inside his jacket pocket.

Inside were six snapshots—all of me! They were taken in *Savvy*'s photo studio, when I was doing the Fashion Flops poses, only thankfully, there weren't any of me in actual garish ensembles. I remembered that day well. Midway through the shoot, I'd tossed my troubles in the reject heap and succumbed to the silly ambiance of it all. These pictures had all been taken when I was fooling around between setups with the other interns. Matt had caught me in the throes of goofiness, cutting up and giggling at the absurdity of the outfits with my peer group.

I started to say, "I had no idea you were taking these," until I realized hello, Matt had gone fully Weegee, capturing me blissfully unaware, in the middle of just being me.

"It's the real you, Cher. Effervescent, bubbly . . ."

Which sounded suspiciously like the commercials for Daddy's antacids until Matt added, "Sweet, generous, and mostly . . . beautiful. These pictures represent the way I honestly feel about you."

"Oh, Matt, this is—" But I was speech-impaired. Matt cupped my chin in his hand, drew me to him, and kissed me tenderly.

We'd made the most of it, but our one and only night together was tragically brief. Matt had to return to his family and his real world in Nebraska. Naturally, we went through the motions of promising to call, beep, fax, and E-mail. But long-distance relationships are like those designer between-season bridge collections. They're all good intentions, but they never reach the emotional heights of the real thing.

As I dropped him by the front door of his apartment, Matt confessed huskily, "You know, Cher, I came to Los Angeles because of a family crisis. But then I met you. You turned out to be the silver lining in our dark cloud. I'll never forget you."

I left him with what I hoped was a kiss to seal that deal.

* * *

I took the scenic route back to Beverly Hills, avoiding the freeways. My thirty days of denial were up, so I was no longer cellularly challenged. Just in time, too, because I so needed to share tonight's bittersweet experience with De. Tragically, she wasn't picking up. I tried paging her, but she must've been stuck in some *X-Files* roaming area or something and couldn't return the call. I punched Murray's digits in, but all I got was his voice mail, punctuated with a headache-inducing hip-hot beat. I was starting to frustrate. I stooped to dial Sean, but even he didn't respond. I was reduced to attempting contact with Amber, but I couldn't even connect with her.

I felt woefully solo. I had my cell phone and my credit cards back, but the hottie of my dreams had vanished in the night. And now my t.b.'s were like, all MIA. Who could I call? Would I resort to Josh? As if! I buzzed Daddy just to make sure my mobile hadn't atrophied, languishing in the no-usage zone. But Daddy picked up right away. And I was massively jubilant at the sound of his comforting voice. Only it turned out that even he was emotionally inaccessible just then. He was all "Just come home, Cher. We'll talk then."

About twenty minutes later, I pulled into our cobblestone driveway. But as I climbed out of my Jeep, something felt deeply askew. Like an Armani A/X mixed in with Emporio Armani. For one thing, the lighting was off—as in turned off. Aside from the halogen floodlights that guided vehicles up our extensive driveway, everything else had gone all power-outagey. From where I stood, it seemed like the entire interior of our bodacious mansion was swathed in complete and utter darkness.

That was odd. Daddy hadn't mentioned he was going out. Even if he was called away unexpectedly, Lucy would still be home. And the beams from her big-screen TV are usually visible from the front of the house.

I felt the hairs on the back of my neck stiffen. No alarm had sounded, but what if there were, like, intruders in the house? I toyed with calling the police. But what would I say exactly? I'm calling to report suspicious . . . darkness? It seemed frivolous, especially when the police force had other pressing matters to attend to like apprehending shoplifters and randoms walking in the streets.

Bravely, I decided to go in. But not without precautions. In a bet-hedging move, I punched 911 on my cellular and positioned the phone so my thumb was poised on Send. Just in case something was fishy when I opened the door, all I had to do was press down. In a last-second flash of defense-mechanism inspiration, I picked up the only weapon at my disposal: a Fendi umbrella. Thus armed, I turned the key and, with my elbow, pushed open the door to my house.

And so like, that's why there exists a video of me, for all future generations of Horowitzes to puzzle over, with a cell phone in one hand, brandishing a way menacing umbrella in another, with a furious deer-in-the-headlights expression on my face. For just as the door swung open, every light in the house burst on, and I was enveloped in a full-tilt boogie chorus of voices squealing, "Surprise!"

The phone and the umbrella crashed to the Italian-tiled floor of our foyer as Daddy, De, Murray, Sean, Amber, and dozens of my nearest and dearest rushed to encircle me. A huge banner hung across the foyer proclaiming Happy Sweet Sixteen, Cher!

For the second time in one night—a record—I, Cher Horowitz, was rendered speechless. And radically teary.

Not to mention befuddled. Like, how could Daddy and my friends have pulled this off without my knowledge? *I'm* the event coordinator in my life. And, last time I looked, in theirs, too!

Daddy put his arm around me and led me into the Great Room, which had morphed into Party Central, festooned with balloons, portable dance floor, juice bar, butler service, and catering by the Cheesecake Factory. A deejay cranked the music up, and all around me couples took to the dance floor, pausing to plant wet ones on my cheek or shake my hand, imparting birthday wishes.

Daddy was all, "If I've been a little distracted lately, now you know why. Organizing a teenage party isn't my strong suit, Cher. Besides, in this house, we rely on you to be the CEO of organizing. It's a good thing you have so many friends who were willing to help."

"But, Daddy," I protested, making my way through the throng, "it's not even my birthday."

"That's true, Cher, and I always felt rotten that we didn't do anything then. But if you remember, you were practicing to get your driver's license, and it was a traumatic time. Now that things have calmed down, I thought, why not?"

"But—but how did you even know I'd be out tonight?" I sputtered.

De sidled up to us and answered, "We were planning to take you out, but then Matt did it for us, so that was a stroke of luck." Then my main big motioned for me to follow her. De led me into the bathroom where, aided by Amber, she began to repair the makeup meltdown that had occurred when I first walked in.

I was still obsessed with finding out how they'd pulled this off in such top-level secrecy. "How and when did you guys have time to plan this?"

Amber was all "Excuse me, like you're the only one who could plan and execute a soirée? Somewhere, Cher, there's a support group for those delusions of grandeur you suffer."

De was all "Amber should know. She's the founding member."

Which inspired us all to high-five.

When I returned to the scene of the gala, it was in full swing. Now that my vision was vibrantly clear, I could see that the invitees were furiously A-list. Aside from my personal posse, I waved hello to Mr. Hall and Miss Geist, and all my worshipers from school. Representatives from my *Savvy* gig were there, too, including Christie and a team of premium interns. Best of all, Vikki was there, and she wasn't alone. In addition to the Warehouse hip-huggers and Express jacket, she was proudly wearing an obviously smitten Rick on her arm. I bounded up to them.

"It's way righteous of you to come, especially after my hard-core bad," I noted sincerely.

Vikki was all, "Don't ever pull anything like that

again, Horowitz, even though, as it turned out, by losing the Brad Bancroft engagement ring slide you actually saved *Savvy* from coming out with an erroneous article."

"So like I could give Alanis lessons in ironic?"

Vikki laughed. "Yeah, I really do think."

Then Rick weighed in. "Vikki's not giving herself any credit. She worked all weekend spin-controlling this crisis. She coordinated the effort between editorial, art, and production, and she got the printers to hold the presses so we could redo the layout." Rick's remarks were aimed at me, but his admiring eyes were riveted to her.

Vikki blushed. "Actually, it worked out well. We had to come up with a new shot of Brad to replace the lost one, and guess who the photographer was?"

I flashed on Matt, who'd been in the photo studio for the Brad shoot.

"The new photo is really different, completely unposed," Vikki was saying. "And Rossman's getting full credit. But don't tell him. I'm going to send an advance copy to his home in Nebraska."

"That is beyond righteous, Vikki!" I burbled. But then I thought about how postal the Celebrities editor, Leggs, must have gone when Vikki told him what happened. "It must have been so not easy mollifying him," I guessed guiltily.

Vikki acknowledged the massive challenge, but she'd risen to the occasion. "I seem to have a way with people." She shrugged.

"You do with *this* person," Rick said, taking her into his arms and guiding her onto the dance floor. As they whirled away from me, Vikki called out, "By the way, Cher, you're welcome to come back to *Savvy*. All is forgiven."

A tempting offer, but I think I've had enough real world experience for like, a decade or so.

All at once, the actual cause of my thirty-day trial run into that world appeared at my side. Josh was all lumberjack chic, Gapped out in plaid flannel and Timberlands, which made me think of Matt. But then Josh flashed his baby blues at me and was all "Come with me. I have some people for you to meet."

As he led me across the room, Josh totally owned up to the results of our bet: Cher–1; Josh–0. "I'm a man of my word, Cher," Josh was saying, as he graciously produced a choice selection of college Baldwins, a blond, a brunet, and a carrot-top, who were all hanging at the juice bar. But as he introduced me, I found myself going on automatic flirt pilot, not even pausing to size up the hottie quotient of any of them.

For the truth was, in another twist of irony? Now that I'd gotten what I'd asked for? I didn't want them anymore. My memories of Matt were too fresh. And hello, unlike some people, I can't just turn my feelings on and off like a faucet. Where had I heard that before?

Whatever. Josh's college hotties didn't go completely unappreciated. There was always Amber. As she twirled on the arm of Baldwin Number One a few minutes later, I tapped her on the shoulder and playfully taunted, "Drooling is a disease that can be licked, Amber."

All at once someone tapped me on the shoulder. It was De, and she was proffering a gift. "There's a bodacious stack of gifts on the table over there," she pointed out, "but I thought you might want to open this one first."

"Dionne! You totally shouldn't have!"

Then Murray bounced over and interjected, "And she didn't have! My woman did not procure this trinket for you."

De bristled. "Put a clamp on it and let me tell her! And if you ever repeat the W word again . . ."

De and Murray fighting? Chronic!

De interrupted her verbal volley to hand me a gift-wrapped box about the size of a Tiffany watch. "This is from someone who couldn't be here tonight."

Gingerly, I unwrapped it. But it was no little hand-big hand bauble. Inside the box sat a webbed artifact that resembled the top half of a tiny tennis racquet, with feathers dangling from the bottom. De nudged me, "Read the card."

"Dear Cher,

When your friends told me they were making you a Sweet Sixteen party, I wanted to be there. But since I couldn't, I got you this. It's a Dream Catcher. According to ancient legend, if you hang it over your bed, it traps all the bad dreams and allows only the sweet dreams to get through. I hope your sweet dreams include me. I know mine will always include you. With love, Matt."

Those last lines were blurry, making them hard to read. I felt myself sliding into serious makeup melt-down again.

But it wasn't only because of what Matt had written. The full import of everything that had happened in the

159

past few weeks totally descended on me. My time with Matt was way *Bridges of Madison County Jr.* The hottie of my dreams had made only the briefest of F-stops into my life. The shutter clicked, and all too soon he was gone.

But then, like Matt's disappearing act, this other feeling enveloped me. It was all, hello, Cher, wake up and smell the cheesecake! I hadn't lost at love. Love is like, all around me. Daddy, De, Murray, Sean, Amber, all my t.b.'s, even Josh. The major effort everyone put in to surprise me with this chronic fiesta? How mushy and love-laden is that?

I heard De and Murray go back to their loving battle when Josh came up behind me. He was carrying a glass of something I couldn't identify.

"Thirsty, Cher?"

"What is this, Josh? It looks like a smog-alert in a glass."

"You don't know? What's the matter, Cher, did you free-fall out of the trend-loop or something? This is wheat-grass juice. It's an antioxidant, antitoxin, immuno-boosting juice. I can't believe you didn't know that. Is it possible I'm more up on the latest crackpot trends than you are?"

"As if!" I bristled, and then had to laugh at what I'd just admitted.

"Just for that, you have to dance with me," Josh said, extending his arms.

"Dance with you? Where's your brainiac girlfriend?"

Josh sighed. "She was never my— Okay, she dumped me. She said that after she thought about it, she realized she could never go out with someone who hadn't made it past the *Jeopardy!* tryouts."

"I'm sorry, Josh," I said sincerely as I put my arm around his neck and we started to dance. The irony of the song didn't escape me. It was that Bryan Adams–Barbara Streisand ballad, "I've Finally Found Someone." Of course, I was massively thinking of Matt as I snuggled comfortably in Josh's arms.

About the Author

Randi Reisfeld is the author of *Clueless: Cher Goes Enviro-Mental, Clueless: Cher's Furiously Fit Workout,* and *Clueless: An American Betty in Paris.* She has also authored *Who's Your Fave Rave? 40 Years of 16 Magazine* (Berkley, 1997); *The Kerrigan Courage: Nancy's Story* (Ballantine, 1994), as well as several other works of young adult nonfiction and celebrity biographies. The Clueless series, duh, is totally the most chronic!

Ms. Reisfeld lives in the New York area with her family. And, grievously, the family dog.

What's it like to be a Witch?

Sabrina
The Teenage Witch™

*"I'm 16, I'm a Witch,
and I still have to go to school?"*

◆◆◆◆◆

#1 Sabrina, the Teenage Witch
by David Cody Weiss and Bobbi JG Weiss

#2 Showdown at the Mall
by Diana G. Gallagher

Based on the hit ABC-TV series

Look for a new title every other month.

**From Archway Paperbacks
Published by Pocket Books**

1345-01

...gs but never bought...